MY BROTHER'S SHADOW

MY BROTHER'S SHADOW

Monika Schröder

FRANCES FOSTER BOOKS

Farrar Straus Giroux

New York

one

I still hear the rhythmic drumming of the rotation press in the printing room of the *Berliner Daily* where I just finished my shift. It's already September, but late summer's humid heat has returned; it clings to me like a hot, wet towel as I walk to the small park across the street and sit in the shade of a linden tree to read the paper I just helped to print. Today's *Berliner Daily* headline boasts "Masterful Retreat at the Ailette Front," announcing the "successful detachment from the enemy." Some people are saying the war is not going as well as the government is trying to make it sound. The newspapers have to print the official armed forces war bulletin so it's hard to know what really is going on, but I am sure the German Reich will achieve final victory.

A woman walks by with a small child on each hand. All three of them look gaunt, their eyes underlined by purplish rings, their cheeks hollow. I'm always hungry myself. After four years of war and the British navy's blockade of German harbors, there is not much left of anything. Printing paper is rationed since last week and the *Berliner Daily* is published on only half the usual number of pages.

On the bottom of the first page I study an advertisement for nerve tonic. It reminds me of Papa, who died at Verdun two years ago. At first his letters proudly described the devastating impact of the German flamethrowers on the enemy's morale, but as the battle dragged on he openly expressed his despair. When my mother read one of those sad letters to us, my older brother, Hans, turned red in the face and yelled, "Maybe we should send him a nerve tonic to build up his strength if he is such a weakling." Hans can get angry like that. It hurt to hear him talk about Papa this way, but I didn't dare say anything.

Soon after, we got the letter informing us that Papa had died. Because he also worked for the *Berliner Daily* the paper paid for his obituary. His name appeared in one of the many black-framed boxes under an Iron Cross, announcing his heroic death on the battlefield for "People, Kaiser, and Fatherland." When I showed it to Mama she threw the paper across the kitchen table and said, "People, Kaiser, and Fatherland? My husband didn't die for me or for his country. He only died for our foolish Kaiser, who loves his uniforms and his yachts. He and his military cronies brought us all this misery." Hans argued with her even then, and I wondered how he could make it sound like it was Papa's fault to have been shot dead by the enemy's artillery fire. But I kept quiet. Later I cut out the obituary, folded it neatly, and placed it in the cigar box, the one that shows a picture of the Kaiser in his uniform on the lid.

Now, for more than a year, Hans has been fighting in the trenches on the Western Front. His last letter arrived two weeks ago, asking us to send him lice powder. How awful to be pestered by the little nits while burrowed in the earth, expecting enemy fire or a gas attack at any moment. But Hans was always stronger than me and not afraid of anything. The day Hans left to meet his battalion at the train station, he got angry with Mama for swearing at the "damn war." Hans said it was an honor to serve the Kaiser, and when Mama saw that he really meant it she cried even more.

On the second page a poetry contest calls readers to "Support the War Effort! Write a patriotic poem to encourage Berliners to give money for the 9th War Bond, 1918." A patriotic poem is about all I can contribute to the war effort. I am only sixteen, too young to enlist. The winner of the contest will receive 500 Marks. I know I won't win, but even if my poem comes in third I will get 200 Marks, enough to buy back my mother's sewing machine. It is still with the fat man in the pawnshop at the corner of Charlottenstrasse.

Mama used to sit under the window in our living room, altering dresses or sewing sailor suits for children, while my little sister, Louise, played with her doll on the floor. Last winter, when Louise started to cough, Mama sold the machine to buy medicine and meat. But then Louise spat blood and two days later she died. Shortly after, my mother went to work in the ammunition factory and began to attend socialist party meetings, talking badly about the Kaiser, blaming him for everything.

During my lunch break I had already composed a few lines: *The Kaiser needs us, the Kaiser leads us. Let's give what we . . .* When I read what I have written out loud, the words leave the hollow sound of an empty can rolling over cobblestones. A good poem expresses the true emotion of the author, my former schoolteacher Professor Blum used to say. There is no doubt that I love the Kaiser and my fatherland, but my feelings don't come across in these sentences. I rip the page from the notebook, crumple it into a tight ball, and throw it in the metal waste bin next to the park bench.

Hans would have already found a way to make enough money to buy back the sewing machine. On Sundays he often returned home with lentils, eggs, or other items you couldn't get even with ration cards. He never told me what he and his friend Otto were up to, but I knew he hadn't bought these things with his salary as a watchmaker at Hoffmann & Nolte. He always made sure I didn't follow him when he met with Otto and the gang. In several letters I've asked Hans if he could put in a good word for me with Otto, and explained why I needed the money. But Hans has never responded. I know that Otto's gang still makes money and finds food since I overheard Emil bragging about it. Emil and his older brother, Robert, another friend of Hans's, are both in the gang.

A voice startles me out of my thoughts. "Moritz, what are you doing out here in the heat?"

Herr Goldmann's lanky body jerks with each step as he pulls his right leg in a stiff limp toward my bench. In spite of the heat he wears a suit. Its jacket seems two sizes too big, and the waistline of his pants is bunched together with a belt.

"Just resting after work, Herr Goldmann."

"Resting sounds like a good idea." He sits down next to me and pulls out a handkerchief from his pocket to dab his forehead. "Air as thick as jelly," he sighs, and shakes his head, sending tiny drops of sweat flying from his dark curls. Herr Goldmann is the only younger journalist left at the *Berliner Daily*. Because of his leg he has not been drafted.

"I was too late this time," he says, and holds up a sheet of paper. "You weren't there, so Old Moser sent me right back out." Herr Goldmann often brings his drafts to the printing room after the deadline. If Old Moser, my boss, isn't paying attention, I squeeze the article into the next edition and Herr Goldmann gives me real cigarettes that I sell on the black market. Old Moser thinks they should have found something for Herr Goldmann to do in the war.

"I didn't know you were also a scribbler." He points to my notebook.

"I'm not, really." I like to write my observations in my journal, but I'm not a good writer. After I finished middle school Papa wanted me to start an apprenticeship in the same printshop he worked in. I had dreamed of being a journalist, but there was no money for further schooling once Papa was drafted. The closest I could get to a career in journalism was at the printing press.

"May I?" Without waiting for my answer he takes the notebook and flips through the pages. "You participated in the contest to replace foreign words?"

"Yes, I did. But I didn't win." Last spring, newspapers had asked their readers to help clean the German language of foreign vocabulary. I had suggested "Holland Gravy" to replace "Hollandaise Sauce." But the person who sent in "Dutch Dip" had won.

"You don't like French words? What about ci-ga-rette?" He widens his dark eyes, giving his birdlike face a comical expression, as he pronounces each syllable with the soft vowels that Berliners usually don't have. I wonder how he can make the foreign words sound this way.

"Tobacco roll sounds just fine to me." I shrug.

"You appear to be very interested in politics," he says, turning another page in my notebook with his tapered fingers.

"I like reading the papers."

"But you also write, yourself. This is a vivid description of the parade at Tempelhof Field last March."

I look down and draw a line in the gravel with the tip of my shoe.

"And you copied parts of the Kaiser's speech celebrating his thirty years as emperor last summer." Herr Goldmann reads the excerpt out loud, perfectly imitating the Kaiser's diction. "This war is not fought around a strategic campaign; this war concerns the struggle between two worldviews: Do we uphold the Prussian-German worldview of justice, freedom, and honor? Or do we succumb to the Anglo-Saxon way of doing things, which means the worship of money?"

"You're good with accents," I say.

"Thanks. That's because my mother was an actress."

"She's not acting anymore?"

"Oh, no! She's dead," Herr Goldmann says.

"I'm sorry."

"She died a long time ago, but thank you." He nods and reads another of my short descriptions of the Kaiser's appearances. "You pay attention to detail. That's important for a good writer!"

"I'm not a good writer."

"Maybe not yet," Herr Goldmann says. "But you know what you have to do to become one. That's the first step!"

I'm not sure how to respond. No one has ever called me a good writer.

"Would you like to come with me?" Herr Goldmann gives the notebook back to me. "I'm on my way to report on a social democratic workers' meeting for tomorrow's edition. Have you been to a socialist gathering?"

"No. I don't care for them," I say.

"The meeting is supposed to be disturbed by the police. We might see some action," he says, and winks an eye. "Or do you need to get home?"

I'm not really interested in a political meeting, but it's still too early to go home and maybe Herr Goldmann will give me another cigarette. I pack up my notebook and follow him as he limps toward the park gate.

"Aren't these meetings illegal?" I ask as we pass a long line of women waiting in front of a butcher's shop on Louisenstrasse.

"They are," Herr Goldmann says. "Since the government has made it illegal to gather and talk about the war, which is what the social democrats mostly do, their meetings are illegal."

We turn onto Lindenstrasse, and I am about to ask Herr Goldmann how he learned about this gathering when he stops in front of a pub. "Here it is"—he points at the sign above the entrance—"the Hot Corner. What a fitting name. It's going to be stifling in there."

We walk past the bar and Herr Goldmann speaks briefly to an older man who sits next to the back door. The man nods and lets us enter. All the windows are closed, most of the net curtains drawn. It is almost too hot to breathe. Clouds of smoke hover over the long tables. I recognize the smell of ersatz cigarettes, made from nettles and dried beech leaves, which most people now have to smoke for lack of real tobacco. The benches are filled with middle-aged men in working clothes, but there are also many women in the audience. A short man with thinning hair and a looping black mustache is speaking from the podium. I follow Herr Goldmann as he makes his way closer to the front. The man at the podium raises his voice when he calls out, "The people are paying the price while the bosses of the war industry are profiteering. It's the little man who suffers the most."

"And the little woman," a female voice shouts from the back of the room.

"Yes, you are right," he continues. "The women are suffering here at home. They are the ones who have to feed their families, while the capitalists exploit them in their ammunition factories. Four years of slaughter, misery, and hunger are enough."

"That is Hugo Haase," Herr Goldmann says. "The leader of the Independent Social Democrats. He's a member of the Reichstag."

When Haase finishes his speech, he introduces the next speaker as a courageous leader of the movement. A woman steps behind the podium and I hold my breath.

"Workers," she addresses the audience, "we are gathered here today to express, once again, our discontent with this war. I have already lost my husband to the war. My oldest son is in the trenches on the Western Front. Many of you have lost husbands, sons, or brothers or soon will if this slaughter doesn't come to an end. We have been tricked into believing in the final victory of our beloved country. But now it is time to end this war!" Some people in the audience cheer.

"This woman has guts," Herr Goldmann says approvingly. He scribbles something on his notepad. I don't respond. I can't tell Herr Goldmann that the woman is my mother.

two

I didn't need to stay until Mama had finished her speech. I know her opinion about the Kaiser, capitalist exploitation, and the war. I've heard it all too many times. But I didn't know that she was now speaking at the party meetings she attends and is considered a leader of the movement. She couldn't have seen me in the darkness of the pub's back room. Right after she began to speak I told Herr Goldmann that I needed to leave and walked back home.

On the stairs to our apartment I meet my sister Hedwig. "Hello," I greet her. "Did you get any bread?"

"Yes," she says, "but only one loaf, even though we had ration cards for three."

I open the front door to our apartment on the top floor. A narrow hallway leads to the kitchen, where Hedwig puts down the bread on the wooden table before she makes a fire in the stove. Hedwig is three years older than me and has the same slender build and light brown hair as Mama. I cannot share my outrage about Mama with her because she is as radical as my mother. Since the strikes in January of this year, she accompanies Mama to the large demonstrations, carrying a sign calling for an end to the war.

Hedwig sits down on the coal box and takes off her shoes. "Look at these hands," she sighs. "They will be webbed before too long." Hedwig works in a laundry. She used to be an apprentice to a ladies' dress shop, but after Papa went off to war, she and Mama had to earn money to support the family.

"Can you put some water on the stove?" she asks. "I've touched enough water for one day."

As I fill the kettle, Hedwig sets the table for four. That means Oma Erma will join us. "Can you go and get Oma?" Hedwig asks.

Oma Erma is Papa's mother. She lives with us in the small room next to our kitchen where she spends most of her time either sitting in her chair or lying in bed. Her long, old-fashioned dresses are mostly black, and she wears them, together with her laced-up boots, even when she stays in bed. Like Papa's, her eyes are pale blue. Her unruly gray hair reminds me of the pads of steel wool we use to clean the typesetting machine. Most days it flows in unkempt layers over her shoulders. Only seldom does she allow Mama to tame it into a braid or a bun. I couldn't say what is worse, having to enter the musty dark room to serve her dinner on a tray or watching her sallow face when she eats with us at the kitchen table. The dusty smell of mothballs makes me breathe through my mouth as soon as I enter her room. When I try to open the window she lets out a shriek. "No! Keep it shut! Flies will come inside."

"Oma, better some flies inside than suffocating."

"I am totally against suffocation. Women shouldn't be allowed to vote."

"Oma, suffocation is when you can't breathe. Suffrage is the fight for women's right to vote."

"That is just one of your mother's crazy ideas." Oma slowly gets up from her chair.

"Hedwig says that you will eat with us, so we can let some air in while you are in the kitchen." I turn back toward the window.

"No!" she yells, now standing right next to me, gripping my arm with her bony fingers so hard it hurts. "The window stays shut! Any news from Hans?" Oma shuffles to her chair at the kitchen table.

"No, Oma. He has not written yet," Hedwig says while helping her to sit down.

"Can you get me my shawl?"

"I don't think you need a shawl. It is very hot," I say.

"But the windows are open and the draft will give me a stiff neck."

"Moritz will get your shawl," Hedwig says, and looks at me.

When I return to the kitchen, Mama has come home.

Her face is flushed and dark patches of sweat stain her blouse under her arms and around the neckline. She pours some water into the enamel bowl and soaks a towel to dab her face. "It's hot out there," she says.

"What is this?" Oma points to the light brown slice of bread that Hedwig has placed on her plate.

"That's bread," Hedwig says.

"Or what they call bread, nowadays," Mama says. Before she sits down at the table she rolls up the sleeves of her blouse. The skin on her hands and arms is tinted yellow from the acid in the ammunition factory. Her hair used to be light brown, but recently it has begun to shimmer greenish. I think about the sewing machine. There are still scratches on the wooden floor at the spot where it used to stand. If I could buy the sewing machine back, she wouldn't have to work in the factory. She could earn money staying at home, mending and darning. Everything would be like it used to be, or almost everything.

"I should show you how to make sweet yeast bread," Oma says, waving her knife in the air. "This one is so dark."

"Once we have wheat flour, eggs, sugar, butter, and yeast again we can bake our own bread," Mama says. I chew slowly on my slice of bread. Even with a thick layer of jam it tastes like paper.

"What kind of jam is this?" I ask.

"It's strawberry," Mama answers.

"Tastes more like strawberry-turnip to me," I say.

"It might be only turnip with red food coloring for all we know. They are now putting turnip into everything," Hedwig says, her face drawn into a disgusted grimace.

"Augusta Victoria will meet me later," Oma says.

"The empress might be busy today," I answer, but Mama shoots me a glance. She doesn't like us to respond to Oma's talk about the royals for fear of making her worse.

"I saw you today, Mama," I say.

"Where?"

"At the meeting in the Hot Corner."

"How did you end up there?" Hedwig asks, and Mama turns to me, her eyebrows raised.

"One of the journalists asked me to come. He wrote about your meeting for the paper," I say.

Mama takes another bite from her bread. "Did you hear my speech?"

"No, I left right when you started."

"How many people were there?" Hedwig asks.

"Maybe eighty," Mama says.

"Any police?" Hedwig asks.

"Not this time," Mama says.

"Was the Kaiser there?" Oma asks.

"No," I say. "He wouldn't have liked what Mama had to say."

"Was he in uniform?"

"The Kaiser is always in uniform when in public. He

must have about five hundred different jackets and hats," Hedwig says. "All these costumes, just like a clown."

"How dare you talk like that." I glare at her.

"Moritz!" Mama warns. "Don't start!"

"What am I starting? It's you who have started to go against the Kaiser. And now *she* is insulting him." I point my finger at Hedwig, who smirks.

"Little brother," she says, bending over the table, looking directly at me. "When will you understand that we will lose this war? We have already lost it. What you are reading in the official reports from the front is all hogwash. It's time to make peace."

"With as much dignity and as little loss as possible," Mama agrees.

"How could the German troops win when their own families have lost faith in them? Don't you feel bad for Hans? I wish he was here to help me talk you out of these things," I say.

"We do care for Hans—and that's why we want him to come home," Hedwig says.

"I worry about Hans, though," Mama says. "In the few letters he has written to us, he makes the war sound like a just endeavor." She shakes her head.

"I remember how proud he was when he left for the station," Hedwig says.

"Is Hans coming home?" Oma asks, moving her head slowly from Mama to Hedwig, but neither of them takes any notice of her.

"If you really wanted to help Germany you wouldn't talk like this and Mama wouldn't join those socialists." I throw the gray bread back on the plate and get up from the table. On the way to the door I grab my bag with the notebook and pen. I will finish the poem. I really need to win the money for the sewing machine.

three

Emil waited for me last night in front of the printshop to deliver Otto's message. Hans must have finally written to him for he wants me to come to the Castle Bridge at nine this morning. I leave the house early, since I don't want to tell Mama where I am going. She always warned Hans not to get involved in any "crooked business" and shook her head when he wouldn't tell her where he got whatever he brought home from his Sunday expeditions. But then she was glad to use it anyway.

A large war flag with the black cross on a white background and the Imperial Eagle in the left corner hangs outside the palace. I lean against the railing along the bridge and look down the broad boulevard. From each of the majestic buildings along Unter den Linden the black, white, and red flag of the Reich still flutters in the wind, left from Sedan Day celebrations that took place last week. The holiday commemorates the battle of 1870, when German troops scored an important victory against the French and captured Napoleon III on the battlefield. When we were younger, the boys on our street used to reenact the famous battle. Otto was always the general who commanded the troops and decided who had to play the hapless French. Hans, as his lieutenant, usually made sure I was one of the victorious Prussians. Some poor chap had to play the French emperor and be dragged across the cobblestones while the bystanders cheered and we, the boy soldiers, whipped him with our toy swords made from sticks. The girls who lived on our street wore white aprons and had folded white napkins marked with red crosses pinned in their hair. These "nurses" were eager to help the wounded soldiers. Hans, with his good looks, was always their most popular patient.

The bells of the cathedral ring, calling churchgoers to service. Filing through the double doors of the dome is a long row of women in dark dresses, middle-aged men in their Sunday suits, and a few soldiers on leave in their gray uniforms. I spot Otto's straw-blond hair from a distance. He crosses the Lustgarten in long strides, followed by Robert and his younger brother, Emil. Otto is tall and solid and reminds me of the wooden nutcracker Mama brings out every Christmas. Just like the painted statue, carved from a cylindrical piece of wood, Otto's massive head sits directly on broad, round shoulders. But in spite of his strong build he doesn't have to join the army.

When the doctors discovered a problem with his heart he was exempted from service.

"Morning," Otto says, and pats my shoulder. "I hope you're ready, Moritz."

"Ready for what?"

"Your brother has asked me to let you become part of the gang. But he didn't tell me to skip the initiation ritual." Otto exposes a row of crooked teeth with a false smile.

"What do I have to do?"

"You will show us that we can trust you and that you have the courage it takes to be one of us, right, boys?" Otto turns to Emil, who nods.

Robert says, "I think he is too young."

"I know, I know," Otto says, frowning as if contemplating a difficult problem. "But he comes highly recommended, as you know. His brother, Hans, is fighting for us against the French thieves and English envy and has asked me to take him on. So there must be hope for this runt." He takes a deep breath. "We'll see."

I follow them across Alexander Square, past the Red Fortress of the police station, toward the Nikolai Quarter. During primary school I was envious of Otto, who got to spend more time with my brother than I did. Hans would walk with me to school, but as soon as Otto joined us at the street corner two blocks down the road I had to fall back a few steps behind them. When Hans let me spend time in the company of his friends I was either teased or treated like a cute puppy.

"Where are we going?" I ask, as we turn into a narrow alley behind Rietmüller's Curtains.

"To my house. It's right here." Otto stops at the carriage gate of an old apartment building. It must once have been painted in a vibrant green, but now its façade is covered with bluish-white blotches like moldy bread. Otto's family moved here after his father was drafted. The gate leads into a yard where we pass a tattered horse stable next to a carriage house before we begin to climb the stairs to the building's side wing. Four flights up, Otto unlocks the door to his family's apartment. In the dark hallway we are greeted by the rancid smell of buttermilk and sauerkraut. I am breathing through my mouth, and to my relief Otto opens the window as we enter the living room.

"Let's hurry," Otto calls. "We have to do this before my family comes home from church." Otto pushes a chair under the windowsill.

"Come here," he orders.

"What are you doing?" I try to keep my voice calm as I step onto the chair, but I can hear the edge of fear in my question. When I look down at the yard vertigo dissolves my vision into a blur of windows and cobblestones.

"I told you," Otto says. "We'll find out if you have what it takes to be one of us."

"Now step onto the windowsill," Robert says, and hands Otto a scarf. Emil leans against the tile oven. When my eyes meet his he quickly looks away. I wonder if they did the same thing to him before he could join them. I step onto the windowsill. As soon as I look down vertigo grabs me and I sway back, holding on to the window frame. I turn around, keeping my back to the void at the other side of the window. Otto, now standing on the chair, covers my eyes with the scarf and ties it in a tight knot at the back of my head. Then he begins to spin me around. I feel the grip of his hands on my shoulders. My heart is pounding in my ears. "Turn, turn, turn around." Robert hums a children's tune.

"And then you jump," Otto says.

"But how do I know which side is the living room?" I ask, now the panic clearly ringing in my voice.

"You won't. That's why we are testing your courage," Otto says, and gives me another turn.

"Now jump," Robert calls.

I am dizzy and cannot tell from which side the voice comes. My thoughts are whirling like water flowing into a drain. I take a step forward and let myself fall.

four

I land on the hardwood floor in the living room and pull the scarf off my face. When my eyes adjust to the light I look into Otto's and Robert's smirking faces.

"You made it," Otto says. "I'll let your brother know that you are in."

I push myself up and straighten my pants.

"Now it's time for Operation Sunday," Robert says. "Do you have the bone?"

"It's here," Emil says, and holds up a canvas bag.

"What are we going to do?" I ask.

"We'll try to earn some extra cash by finding goods that are hard to get these days," Robert says.

"*Finding* them . . . That's nicely put." Otto chuckles. "Let's start *searching*."

As we walk along Poststrasse the tolling of the bells at Nikolai Church signals the end of Sunday service. Congregation members line up to shake the minister's hand when they leave.

"What's in the bag, Emil?" I whisper as we turn the corner to Eiergasse.

"I think it's a piece of horse's leg," he says.

"Why do we need a bone?"

"I don't know. They don't tell me much either," Emil says.

We stop in front of a store with a sign that reads BAKERY BLUM in spiky cursive letters. From a black rod above the door hangs a gold-painted pretzel, and the Imperial flag is draped over the empty display case in the window. A brick wall surrounds the bakery's backyard. The gate is closed and locked with a rusty padlock. When I try to peek through a gap between the boards the loud bark of a dog startles me.

"That's why we need the bone," Otto says.

"We'll throw him the bone and then climb over the wall," Robert says as we retreat far enough from the gate to make the dog calm down.

"But won't he want to bite us more than he likes running after the bone?" I ask.

"We'll see," Otto says. "That's why we brought you. You will stay in the yard to watch the dog and, if needed, distract him from us."

"How will you get inside the bakery?" Emil asks anxiously.

"I checked out the back door yesterday when the gate was open," Otto says. "It has a lock that should be easy to break with a screwdriver. And I brought one."

"We'll get into the basement and carry the flour out. I know it's there since I saw the delivery on Friday," Robert adds.

"So we will be *finding* flour?" Emil asks.

"Exactly." Otto nods. "And you will stand out here and whistle if somebody comes. Let's go."

I wish I could trade jobs with Emil, but I don't dare ask. I follow Robert and Otto as they pull themselves up the wall, glad that I can do it in one swing and don't have to wait for one of them to give me a hand. As soon as the dog sees us he starts to bark again. He jumps up the wall, exposing his teeth in a snarl. Robert throws the bone to the far corner of the yard. The dog follows the bone and catches it in his fangs. Then Robert and Otto jump down and hurry to the door. I push myself off the wall. For a moment the dog's ears perk up when he sees me in the yard. The hair on the back of his neck is standing up. He lets out a dark growl and I wonder how quickly I can climb the wall should he decide to come after me. But then the dog lowers himself to the ground and begins to gnaw on the bone without taking his eyes off me, responding with a growl to my every move. I freeze. From the corner of my eye I see that Otto and Robert have opened the door and have disappeared into the basement. I hear the bone splinters cracking between the dog's jaws. Before long Otto comes out, bags of flour in each hand. Robert follows shortly with a similar load. "Okay," Otto calls. "Let's go." He reaches the wall first, puts down the bags before he pulls himself up. "Pass me the bags!" he yells down to us. I rush toward the wall. "Hurry!" Otto calls while Robert stretches himself, passing his bags to Otto. "The dog won't stay there forever!" As soon as my fingers have found a firm grip at the top layer of bricks I can hear the dog snapping behind me. Robert pulls himself up without trouble, but I feel the tug on the leg of my pants. When I try to shake the dog off with a swift kick I hear my pants tear. A sharp whistle cuts through the air. "Moritz!" Emil warns from the other side of the wall. "You have to hurry!" I push the tip of my shoe against the wall and pull myself up. As I reach the other side I have to run to catch the others, who rush down the alley toward the river.

five

I turn around but no one follows us. *Thief, thief, thief.* The words echo in my head. Now I know what my brother used to do on Sundays and I am a criminal, too. When the baker returns to his bakery later today, the remaining flour will make even fewer loaves and more people will leave the queue outside his store without any bread. I wipe these thoughts away and force myself to think of the sewing machine and how glad Mama will be to have it back. Otto leads us to a shed by an abandoned boat dock near the bridge over the river Spree, where we lean against the back wall, catching our breath. On the other side of the river the Imperial Palace looms in the distance.

I'm glad I brought a canvas bag to carry my loot. Otto divides the flour equally among the four of us before we get ready to leave.

"We'll let you know the time and place for the next operation," Otto says.

"What are we going to do then?" I ask.

"It's better you don't know too much in advance. Let me worry about the logistics!" Otto says.

~~~

I wish I could bring the flour home to Mama and Hedwig. Mama could bake her own bread or even make a cake. But what would I say if they asked how I got four bags without weekly ration cards? Bakers are not allowed to sell flour without food stamps and we used ours already. I need more money for the sewing machine, so I decide I better sell the flour. I pass a small square where a few older men and women stand beside their carts, offering fruits and vegetables from their own gardens for exorbitant prices. I stop and ask one of them if she would like to buy some flour. She looks at me skeptically and asks me to show her the packet. When I do she offers me six potatoes for two packages. "No, I need money," I say. She shakes her head and makes a dismissive gesture with her hand. "No, my boy," she says. "Money I can't give you."

I try again with a man whose left sleeve is tucked into his jacket. Maybe a veteran will give me money in exchange for my loot. But he offers eggs in return. I finally approach a bearded old man in a black coat who sits on a low stool in front of a grocery store, looking at me expectantly. Spread out in front of him is a small black-and-white blanket with several watches on display. His hat covers a thatch of thick gray hair and I notice a corkscrew lock dangling in front of each of his ears. The watches remind me of Hans, and among the old man's collection I see one that looks similar to the watch Hans wears. The old man smiles at me and says, "Beautiful time-pieces! Which one do you like?" But I shake my head and ask if he would like to buy flour.

"Yes, yes, yes! God must have sent you my way. How much flour do you have?"

"Four packages."

"Four packages!" The old man rubs his hands together. "Am I a lucky Jew! How much do you want for them?"

"Eight Marks per bag," I say.

"You want to cheat me?" He has gotten up from his stool and now looks at me, his eyes widened dramatically.

"Seven," I say.

"How about I give you twenty-five for all four?" he says, and pulls the bills from his pocket.

In the reflection of the storefront window I see two policemen walking onto the square. "Here." I pass him my bag. "Give me twenty-five Marks and then we'll both have to run." I motion behind me and he nods. With a swift movement he rolls the watches into the blanket and stuffs them into a leather bag. He presses the bills into my hand, lifts his hat, and says, "Thank you, boy," before he hurries away.

six

A week later, Herr Goldmann is waiting for me outside the printshop after I finish the early shift. "Any news from your brother?"

"No letter yet," I say.

He offers me one of his real tobacco cigarettes. I take it and slip it into my shirt pocket. "Thank you."

"How long has it been since the last letter came?"

"I worry that something happened to him. We haven't heard from him for more than three weeks."

"I'm sure your brother will write soon," he says, and lights himself a cigarette. "You took off so quickly from the meeting at the Hot Corner on Saturday," he continues. "But you didn't really miss anything. It was just the usual speech against the war and the emperor, this senseless slaughter and the profiteering of industrial giants like Krupp and Stinnes, and so on." He makes me laugh as his voice trails off in a parody of Hugo Haase's East Prussian accent. But then he suddenly turns serious. "I shouldn't make fun of them," he says. "They're right. It's time for all this to be over."

"Do you think we will lose the war?" I ask.

"It's only a matter of time until Bulgaria capitulates. Austria, for whom we started this mess in the first place, has already thrown in the towel. Even Ludendorff finally admits that he is losing the war," Herr Goldmann says, and takes a drag from his cigarette. "Don't look so shocked, boy. Surely you know that the armed forces report that we have to print every day is not telling the truth."

"How could all of this have been for nothing?" I ask.

"That's what happens when people follow their leaders blindly," Herr Goldmann says, and blows out a plume of smoke. "Do you remember August 1914? Everyone cheered when the Kaiser declared war. The soldiers left on the trains westward accompanied by music and women waving from the sidewalk. The Kaiser promised the troops would be home 'before the leaves have fallen from the trees' and would celebrate Christmas at home." He stops to shake his head. "The leaves have fallen four times since then," he says quietly.

"But don't you feel the need to support our troops?" I ask.

"My brother returned from France two months ago. He has not been shot nor has he lost a limb, but he is an invalid nevertheless," Herr Goldmann says. "I've kept all his letters he sent from that hell, describing the realities and horrors in detail. There is nothing glamorous about battle."

"How is he an invalid?" I ask.

"He has a constant shiver. The doctors say it's a nerve condition. He's thin as a rail and shakes all the time. My sister-in-law finally had to send him to a clinic for war veterans. Fortunately, her family had the money to pay for his care," Herr Goldmann says.

I don't know what to say, so I look down at my shoes and bury my hands deeper into my pockets.

"Where are you going now?" Herr Goldmann asks.

"I was going to go to the main office to see if they need someone to sell the *Berliner Daily* anywhere here in the district."

"I think I have a better idea," Herr Goldmann says. "Why don't you try writing a piece for the paper? The editor is always looking for new talent."

"I don't think I'm a new talent." I shrug.

"You need to stop focusing on the things you're not," he says. "You read the papers regularly. You know the style. I saw your writing. Why don't you take my next assignment?"

"What's your next assignment?"

"The editor in chief wants an article about the lawsuit against the Duchess von Bülow. So I have to be at the District Court in twenty minutes. But I just found out that this afternoon in Charlottenburg there will be another workers' meeting, outside the Siemens factory. I cannot be in two places at the same time. I thought you could go there and cover it."

"Really?"

"Really! If this doesn't interfere with your schedule in the printshop I would very much like you to go there and write the article for us."

"I finished my shift for today. How much do you pay?"

"Now you are talking like a real journalist!" He winks an eye. "They pay five pfennig per line. Such an article brings about two Marks."

This time Mama won't be at the demonstration. She told us in the morning that she needed to work a double shift at the factory.

"Thanks," I say. "Where do I bring the draft?"

"Bring the draft around six to the newsroom," Herr Goldmann says as he sets off toward the subway.

I cannot believe my luck. Herr Goldmann asked me to write for the *Berliner Daily*! And they will even pay me money for it. I can't wait to mention this in my next letter to Hans. He will be so proud.

seven

From the streetcar I can already see a crowd in front of the Siemens factory. When I cross the tracks a young woman with the same greenish hair as Mama's hands me a flyer that reads: "Stop the production of war ammunition and weaponry! Strike with us!" I want to return it to her but then remember that I came here as an observer and should pay attention to detail, so I stuff it in my pocket.

A group of women, many still in their dirt-streaked working aprons, walk out of the factory gate and join the demonstrators. Just as at the meeting in the back room of the Hot Corner, the men who attend the demonstration are mostly older or too young for military service. Some of them hold signs calling to "End the War!" and for "Bread and Peace!" A skinny young man dressed in the checkered pants of a baker's apprentice climbs up a lamppost for a better view. I make my way to the front of the crowd, where a bench next to a kiosk serves as a podium for the speaker, a bespectacled man in a workman's jacket. When I reach the kiosk I hear his raspy voice: "Curse the Kaiser, the Kaiser of the rich. He can't know our misery. He won't rest until he exacts the last drop from us and lets us be shot like dogs!" The crowd responds with approving applause. I take out my notebook to write down what he says and copy the slogans on the signs. As I crane my neck to estimate the number of people assembled, the speaker finishes his speech with a fiery shout of "End this war now!" echoed by the crowd.

A familiar voice addresses the demonstrators next, and I can't believe my eyes when I see Mama has climbed onto the bench. She stands slightly bent forward, the backs of both hands pressed against her waist, forming two triangles with her arms. Her eyes are focused on a spot near the back of the crowd. Her voice sounds firm, not shrill, as she calls for an "immediate strike to force the government to make peace."

Suddenly, hooves clack on the cobblestones. Two policemen on horseback approach the crowd. They stop their horses next to the lamppost from which the young baker's apprentice shouts, "Get away from us! We have the right to speak freely!" A white-haired man in a dark blue cap shakes his fist at the police. One of the uniformed men presses his heels into his horse's side, forcing it to step forward, trying to disperse the crowd. But the demonstrators do not move. Instead, more of them shake their fists and yell at the policemen, whose faces now show fear. Mama continues to speak. She calls the Kaiser "vain" and "out of touch with reality," words I don't need to write down since I've heard them before and I know that I will remember them.

I look down the street, expecting more policemen to appear. The horses shake their heads nervously and foam forms around their bits. With a swift move, the boy on the lamppost reaches down and pulls one policeman's helmet off his head. The men closest to him cheer and encourage him to throw it out to the crowd. When the helmet flies across the audience the policeman tries to grab the boy's leg. But the boy quickly slides down the lamppost and jumps to aid the man in the blue cap as he pulls the policeman off his horse. The horse gallops away while the second mounted policeman hurries to rescue his colleague. Mama stops her speech. More policemen arrive, pushing their way closer to the bench. One of them calls, "Catch her. She is Anna Schmidt. She's the rabble-rouser who insulted the Kaiser. This is treason!" I want to rush to help Mama, but she has already disappeared, and I am trapped between the kiosk and the stream of demonstrators who are now running in all directions. I search the crowd, trying to see if the police have taken Mama into custody, but the men in uniform seem to have lost sight of her. They look at each other and shrug. With a loud rumble and screeching, the next streetcar stops at the station. I see Mama run up the stairs and reach the platform just as the car begins to move. A man's arm reaches out from the closest compartment and pulls her in. The doors close and the streetcar slowly rolls away. Mama has escaped.

eight

I almost miss my stop at Friedrichstrasse station where I have to switch trains. My mind keeps going back to the moment Mama disappeared into the streetcar compartment. The policeman calling her name echoes in my head. I sit down on a bench, trying to calm my breathing before I write the article. Three trains come and go but I am still sitting in front of an empty page. The police knew her name so they can easily find where she lives. Why was she even there and not at work? I finally begin to write, describing the location of the demonstration, the kinds of people who attended, and the slogans on their signs. What would Hans say if he knew about this? In my letters I have told him about the meetings Mama goes to and what she and Hedwig say at home about the war, but he never makes any comment about Mama's political activities in his letters to us.

Herr Goldmann said that the article should only be 260 words long, just a short notice about another illegal demonstration broken up by the police. I add a few descriptive sentences before I write my ending: "The demonstration was dissolved by the police. The female speaker got away before the police could catch her."

Herr Goldmann has not returned to the office when I arrive. Another journalist shows me his desk, where I leave a note together with my article before I hurry home.

~~~

The door to our apartment is wide open. Men's voices are coming from the kitchen, and I can hear Oma whining in her room. Hedwig is talking to a stout policeman whose eyes are too small for his round, puffy face and whose flat, short nose resembles a pig's.

"She has not come home," Hedwig says. "I've told you already several times!"

"What is going on here?" I ask.

"We're looking for your mother, Anna Schmidt," the policeman says. "Do you know where she is?"

"No," I say, and look at Hedwig, who shrugs.

A second policeman, this one tall and skinny with a pencil-thin mustache, enters the kitchen.

"Close the curtains! I have a headache!" Oma complains from her bedroom.

"One of us will wait at the door downstairs," the first policeman says. "Your mother will come home eventually."

"What did she do?" Hedwig asks.

"She spoke at an illegal demonstration and insulted the Kaiser," the taller policeman says, his upper lip stretched into a line as thin as his mustache. "She will be indicted for treason and insulting the emperor!"

"Günter, let's go!" the first policeman says, and walks toward the hallway. "We'll get her one way or another."

After we hear the front door close, Hedwig rushes into Oma's room and closes the curtains and her door before she sits down at the kitchen table.

"I saw Mama," I say, taking a seat across from her. "She was at the demonstration at the Siemens factory, calling for a strike and demanding an end to the war."

"Did you see her leave?"

"When the police came she disappeared. Then I saw a man pull her into the streetcar before the police could catch her."

"That's good!" Hedwig massages her face with both hands.

"I thought she was working a double shift," I say.

"She was going to, but then they asked her to come to this spontaneous demonstration and she traded with someone at the factory. I will take Mama her bag," Hedwig says.

"You know where she is?"

"She expected that eventually the police would come after her. That's why she kept a bag with a change of clothes under her bed."

"But how do you know where she is?"

"That was part of the plan. She needed a place to hide in a situation like this."

"Where?"

Hedwig looks at me. "Can I trust you?"

"You think I would turn in my own mother?"

"The way you usually talk about her involvement in the movement doesn't make us feel that you are a supporter."

"I'm not a supporter. I wish she wouldn't do this," I say. "And neither should you. I wish the two of you wouldn't say all these things about the Kaiser and that we are losing the war . . ."

Hedwig holds up the palm of her hand. "Let's not start this now!"

"Where is she? You have to tell me. I won't tell the police."

"At Aunt Martha's," Hedwig says.

I'm not surprised. Aunt Martha is Mama's unmarried older sister, a teacher in a girls' school and a high-ranking member in the German Women's League, where she fights for women's right to vote. I remember her last visit to our house, at Christmas in 1915, when she and Papa got into an argument. She called him a "pigheaded patriarch" and left before we exchanged presents.

"How will you take the bag to her if there is a policeman waiting downstairs? He will assume that you know where she is and follow you," I say.

"You're right," Hedwig says. "But what are we going to do?"

"I have an idea! We'll pack a second bag for her and leave together. The policeman will follow us. Then we split up at the intersection."

"What is that supposed to do?"

"The policeman can only follow one of us. He has to make a choice and if he follows me you'll take the bag to Mama. If he follows you I'll go to Aunt Martha and you lead the policeman somewhere else."

"That's a smart idea." Hedwig smiles. "I'll pack a second bag while you take Oma some dinner."

"No!" I say. "I already had the smart idea. You should take Oma her supper."

nine

When we leave through the main entrance the policeman with the pig face is standing on the sidewalk. We greet
him as we pass, he nods, and just as expected, he follows
us. We stop at the intersection where we have agreed to
go on in different directions. When we split up the policeman follows Hedwig. I wait for a short while in front of
the subway entrance to make sure that he really is gone
before I take the train to Charlottenburg, where Aunt
Martha lives in one of the newer apartment houses with
wrought-iron balconies on the front and a stone relief
above the front door.

The steps on Aunt Martha's broad, wooden staircase
are covered with carpet. I climb past stained-glass windows that show women with wavy red hair in long flowing
dresses. I have to ring the doorbell twice before I hear
footsteps inside.

"It's your boy!" Aunt Martha calls, and lets me in. Aunt Martha has the same willful eyes as Mama and looks at me skeptically from her imposing height.

Mama is standing at the end of the corridor. "Moritz!"

I run toward her and let myself sink into her arms. It feels good to breathe in her scent and for a moment I forget that I am angry at her. But when she lets go of me I look right at her and ask, "Why are you doing this?"

"Doing what?"

"Insulting the Kaiser in public, committing treason, betraying Hans and Papa by not believing in our victory."

"Moritz," she says mildly, and pulls me into the living room. "Come and sit down."

I follow Mama and take a seat on the crimson sofa. The opposite wall is covered with bookshelves. Mama sits down in one of the wing chairs next to the sofa which are also upholstered in the same berry-colored velvet. Dark red curtains frame the windows. I had forgotten Aunt Martha's love for the color red but now I remember Papa's comment when we left her apartment after one of our rare visits. "It looks like the boudoir in a whorehouse!" Mama had shot him a glance followed by a sharp "How do you know what those look like, Gustav?"

"Has your son joined the Fatherland Party?" Aunt Martha asks now, walking over to her sideboard. "Anna, you really should have been stricter with this boy's education." She looks down at me with a mocking expression before she takes a third cup out of her sideboard and places it on the coffee table in front of me.

"Have some coffee," Mama says, and fills my cup.

"The police are looking for you. They searched the apartment and placed a policeman outside our house. We split up to confuse him as to who will come to see you. You cannot come home or they'll arrest you." The sentences shoot out of me.

Mama listens calmly. I want to tell her how hurt I was that she hadn't told me about her plan. But I keep quiet for fear of hearing Mama say that she hadn't been sure she could trust me. Just thinking about it brings back the pang I felt when Hedwig talked about their doubts earlier. I study the poster on the back of the door for International Women's Day, March 8, 1914, with a woman waving a red flag above bold black letters demanding women's right to vote.

"We knew this would happen, Moritz. Of course, we hoped that it wouldn't, but now I'll stay here with Martha."

"For how long?"

"Until all of this is over," Mama says.

"What is over?"

"Moritz." Aunt Martha has sat down in the other wing chair. She bends slightly forward the same way Mama does when she wants to support her argument. "This government is bankrupt. They have misled the people for four years, promising that they will win the war, while exploiting the poor workers and women." I remember what Herr Goldmann said, but it's different when it comes from Aunt Martha. "The Kaiser has to go. Germany must be a democracy. Women must be allowed to vote. That is also one of the allies' conditions for peace. You read the papers, boy! You know that this autocratic regime is over!" She leans back in her chair, and I assume that she has finished her lecture. A silence fills the room and I take a sip of the bitter chicory coffee.

"If you can't go to work, how will you earn money?" I finally ask Mama.

"There is a construction company here in the neighborhood. Martha says they're looking for workers. I'll go there tomorrow."

"A construction company?" I try to imagine Mama carrying heavy loads of bricks.

"I'm a strong woman," Mama says, and flexes the muscles of her arms jokingly.

"Strong enough to be exploited by war profiteers in an ammunition factory," Aunt Martha adds. "Haven't you noticed that as soon as the patriarchy needs women it becomes accepted that we work in factories, drive streetcars, and clean garbage bins? But the right to vote in an election they deny us, as if we are children!"

Mama shoots her a warning glance not to begin another lecture.

"I'll bring you the ration cards when they come out this week," I say.

"Keep them for yourselves. You won't be able to come here too often anyway. Eventually the police will find out where you're going. And please take good care of Oma," Mama says.

"What if the police do come here?" I ask.

"Then we have this." Aunt Martha gets up and opens the top drawer of her sideboard. When she turns around she is holding a revolver. The expression on her face shows me that she is determined to use it.

ten

"It's not the people's place to chase away a king." Old Moser, my boss, has to yell over the noise of the printing press.

"A king who kills his own people with war and starvation?" Mahlke, the journeyman, hollers from the other side of the printshop.

"This war was started to defend us against the French!" Old Moser calls back.

"This war was started because we had an alliance with a senile Austrian emperor and because our own Kaiser wanted to show off his naval power against his British cousins!" Mahlke bellows.

It's always like this when they have the same shift. At some point Old Moser and Mahlke start to argue. If Old Moser and I work with Plattner, the other journeyman, there is hardly any conversation, since Plattner has no interest in politics. But Old Moser and Mahlke seem to enjoy this bickering as they are standing on either side of the press, their reddened faces shiny from sweat and the heat of their arguments. Mahlke, tall with stooped shoulders, pulls out his handkerchief to dab his bald head. Old Moser has kept his sturdy frame in spite of the food rationing. His wife works in the dairy at Bolle's and must be bringing extra rations home for her family. Now he scratches his reddish-gray curls and declares that it's time for a short break.

I sit down next to Mahlke by the window. He has a thermos with tea and offers me a cup. Old Moser smells his sandwich suspiciously before he takes a bite. Then he spreads out the morning edition of the paper.

"So they've made Prince von Baden chancellor now," he says.

"What difference does that make?" Mahlke asks. "The Kaiser appointed his cousin to be chancellor. It all stays in the family."

Old Moser shakes his head. "It's sad that it had to come to this."

Mahlke says, "It's about time that it comes to this. But your head is as hard as General Hindenburg's. You'll never change."

"Are you one of these radicals now?" Old Moser asks.

"I'm no radical, just more enlightened than you, old hardhead," Mahlke says. He shakes his head as he screws the top back on his thermos. Old Moser crunches the wrapping paper of his sandwich into a ball and tosses it into the basket next to the printing press. Then he turns the page of his paper. I look out the window, where a crow has landed on a branch of the linden tree in the courtyard. I've heard that the new chancellor, even though he is the Kaiser's cousin, plans to begin armistice negotiations with the allies. It does look like the war is lost. But at least when it's over, Hans will come home.

"How did *you* get in here?" Old Moser says, and holds up page three, where my article is printed in the lower left corner of the morning edition. I am beaming to see my name in print.

"Herr Goldmann asked me to write about this demonstration," I say, expecting a compliment from my boss for my smooth writing. They have made almost no changes to my draft and the cashier gave me the two Marks Herr Goldmann had promised.

"Why do you think he sends you to these events?"

"Because he likes me," I say.

"Is that what he says?" Old Moser looks at me, frowning.

"He says that I write well, that I have talent," I say.

"Even the quickest bird is caught with flattery," Old Moser says.

"I'm earning a little extra money with the articles," I say, still trying to defend myself.

"Just don't forget where you belong, boy," Old Moser says, and gets up to start the press again.

eleven

A week later, Otto sends Robert to tell me to come to Schlesisches station the following Sunday. By the time I arrive Otto is already waiting for me in front of the ticket booth. It is one of those blustery early autumn days when the Berlin sky hangs low, covering the city with a gray blanket of clouds that spew rain at intervals.

"Where are the others?" I ask.

"They're working on another operation today. You and I will pay a visit to a distant cousin of my mother who owns a farm in Tarmow, to get some fresh food," he says as we join the queue.

"What do we need the cart for?" I ask, pointing to the hand wagon next to Otto filled with old tires.

"Moritz, Moritz." Otto shakes his head. "Always too many questions from you, young man."

The train is packed, but we get the last two seats on a

wooden bench in the third-class compartment. Otto dozes off as soon as the train starts moving, while I watch the city slowly passing by on the other side of the window. I worry about what kind of crime we will commit today. Now I wish I had told Emil that I had to take a Sunday shift and wouldn't be able to come. But I need the money. Are we going to break into his aunt's basement? I have read how farmers now use weapons to protect themselves against the starved city folk who come in droves to trade or buy food.

By the time we get out at the Tarmow train station the worry has grown into a knot in my stomach. Otto seems in a royal mood and whistles as we walk along a treelined cobblestone street to enter the village of Tarmow.

"Here it is," Otto says, and stops in front of a small brick farmhouse. The roof is covered with black slates that glisten from the last rain shower.

"She's probably out in the back. Let's go around."

The rusty gate gives in to our push with a loud squeak. We walk past the house into a narrow backyard, framed by a low stable on the right and a barn to the left. Across the cobblestone yard is a garden, fenced off with rolls of barbed wire.

"Look at this!" I say. "They're protecting their garden with the same barbed wire they use in the trenches."

"I'd do the same if I had a garden and all these city people came every weekend begging for food, or stealing it," Otto says. "Hello!" he shouts.

His call is answered by the deep bark of a large dog.

"Oh, no!" I say, ready to bolt.

"Don't worry! She keeps him on a leash."

"Who's there?" A tall woman steps out from the stable, cradling a rifle in her arms.

"It's me, Otto! And I brought my friend Moritz, just like I told you last time."

The woman steps closer and studies me skeptically. Her full figure indicates that she has no trouble feeding herself in times of war. The tips of wooden clogs peek from under the mud-stained hem of her apron.

"Don't stare at my clogs!" she yells. "One of you city folks brought me leather boots in exchange for food!" She wipes a wisp of her hair off her forehead. "Hah! The boots looked nice and fit well, but after the first rain they completely dissolved. Turns out they were made from papier-mâché covered with a thin veneer to fool me!" She shakes her head. "City folk! Bah! All robbers and charlatans!"

"I'm sorry to hear that, Aunt Mimmi," Otto says.

"So he's the one?" She points at me.

"Yes. He can do it. I'm sure."

"All right, then." She motions with the rifle. "Come with me!"

"Where are we going?" I ask as she leads me behind her barn.

"You'll help me harvest my potatoes," she says, and points to a potato field, also surrounded by spirals of barbed wire.

"How do we get in there?"

"Here!" She points to a pitchfork on a nail on the barn wall. "You can lift it with this. And here is a basket."

I manage to push the pitchfork under the barbed wire and lift it up. Then I throw the basket ahead of me and crawl through on all fours. "You know how to harvest potatoes?" she calls from the other side of the wire. "Pull up the plants by their stems, shake the tubers, and place the potatoes carefully in the basket!"

"I know, I know!"

"I'll be back in one hour. You can keep half of whatever you harvest," she says, and walks away.

I am relieved that we are working for food and won't have to steal it. I like the smell of fresh soil and work quickly. Soon my hands are muddy, and when I come closer to the end of the next row I pause to look up at the spiral of barbed wire. In one of his early letters Hans described his view from the trenches. I wonder where Hans is right now, if he is looking through the barbed wire across a stretch of no-man's-land to the fields of northern France. Something scurries away. I see a field mouse disappear behind a mound of soil. Hans also described the rats in the trenches and added a photograph of himself with one of the terriers the soldiers train to catch the vermin. I shudder, thinking about having to sit in a muddy trench, afraid for one's life, fighting rats and lice. Then I force myself to start the next row.

――――

――――

――――

――――

――――

――――

――――

When Aunt Mimmi calls me to come back, Otto is waiting for me in the yard. "What did you do while I was harvesting potatoes?"

"He helped to make butter," Aunt Mimmi says. "I don't get much help around here. My son and husband have fallen in Russia and my daughter is in the hospital with a high fever from the Spanish flu." For a moment the harsh expression on her face melts and her eyes get cloudy. But then I see the rifle leaning against the stable door and the tender moment for Aunt Mimmi passes.

"I stuck some sausage and rolls of butter into the tires in the cart," Otto says. "Now you know why we needed the cart. The policeman at the station will check the returning passengers for smuggling food. One needs to be inventive."

"One also needs to come with a partner who is not such a wimp as the boy you brought last month," Aunt Mimmi says. "He was so frightened the policeman saw right through him and took away all the food." She shakes her head and snorts.

"That was Emil," Otto says. "He's not cut out for this kind of work. That's why I brought Moritz this time."

"What if they have dogs? They would sniff the food right away," I say.

"They are not that smart. It's the police after all," Otto says, and makes a dismissive gesture with his hand.

"Have a sandwich before you go." Aunt Mimmi offers us each a thick slice of bread smeared with butter. I can't believe this is *real* bread. I chew slowly and savor the taste before I swallow. "Thank you!" I say to her before we leave the yard. "Don't get caught!" she calls after us, and Otto salutes her with a quick touch to his brow.

On the train back to Berlin I look at the other passengers, wondering if they are hiding food under their clothes or in their bags. I've heard girls sew food into their petticoats since the police don't dare to check there. This time I will keep part of the loot for Mama and Hedwig. If they ask where I got the potatoes, I can tell them that I went to help Otto's aunt with her harvest. That is not even a lie.

When we arrive at Schlesisches station the police are waiting for us. They block the entrance to the stairwell and won't let any passenger leave the platform without a check of their luggage.

"Now they'll catch us," I say to Otto, imagining how we will be led away in handcuffs.

"Hush!" Otto says as a skinny policeman motions us to lift the tarp.

"Just old tires," Otto says.

"Did you have to go out in the country to find those?" the policeman asks.

"My uncle has a carriage business. He lets me take the rubber to the resource collection station in Tiergarten. He lost his leg, so he's glad for me to do it."

I just stand there and nod.

"Hey, Erich! We need Rex over here," the policeman calls to his colleague on the other side of the staircase. Erich nods, and through the crowd of people I see him coming toward us with a large black dog on a leash. The dog seems very excited as he approaches the cart. His stubby tail wiggles and with one jump he is standing on top of our tires, digging his nose deep down. "He found something!" the skinny policeman says. The dog starts to bark and pulls a sausage out from the tires. "Well, boys! It's against the law to obtain food without ration cards," the man who's holding the dog says. "Rex, down! Let's see what else they have in there." The policeman pulls the dog away and his colleague begins to rummage through the cart. When he has uncovered all our food he turns to us and says, "You're free to go, but we'll confiscate the cart."

"Looks like the police are smarter than you thought," I whisper to Otto as we leave the station. He averts his eyes and mumbles, "I wish we had eaten the sausage on the train."

twelve

The following Sunday I am surprised to see Emil waiting for me outside the printshop after my morning shift. "Otto wants you to come to the Roland Fountain in Tiergarten at four," he says, and turns around to leave.

"What are they planning now?" I ask. "We just went out of town last week."

"I heard that operation failed," Emil says. "Otto has a new plan."

"I don't think I'll have time," I say. "That's just in another two hours."

Emil looks at me, the bridge of his nose crinkled like he took in a bad smell. "I wouldn't say that if I were you," he says.

"What do you mean?"

"Now you're part of the gang. So you better do what

Otto says. You can't pick and choose which operations you'd like to be part of."

"But I don't want to steal," I say.

"It's too late to back out now. Your brother wanted you to be part of the group and Otto let you in. It's only a reconnaissance mission anyway," he says. "The real sting will be next weekend. See you later." He lifts his hand to wave goodbye before he walks away.

On my way to the Roland Fountain at the entrance to the Tiergarten Park I worry that Emil may have told Otto about my hesitation. But Otto just tells us to follow him and leads us up Tiergartenstrasse and stops in front of one of the large villas.

"This is it," he says.

"How do you know that no one is at home?" I ask.

"My sister works here. She told me that the family has left the city for fear their children will contract the Spanish flu," Otto says.

"And she gave you the key?"

"She didn't *give* it to me." Otto grins. "I *borrowed* it for the evening."

He unlocks the gate and we follow him up the gravel path to the main door. The two-story house is made from red-brown brick. Tall narrow windows are set above massive granite windowsills. I feel safer once we have entered the well-tended garden and walk behind a row of conifers that shelter us from the street.

"These people like their privacy," I say, and point to

the canopy of a majestic beech tree that spreads out its purple leaves over the left side of the house.

"That's good for us," Emil agrees, still turning back nervously to the gate. His shoulders are pulled together, giving away his worry about being caught. Otto opens the heavy front door and we enter the vestibule.

"What's that smell?" I ask.

"That's the smell of money," Robert answers, and smirks at me as we walk through the front hall into the living room.

"It smells like vinegar and something else, maybe cough drops," Emil says.

"My sister said that they fumigate the whole house twice a week against the Spanish flu," Otto explains.

"So we won't get sick in here," Robert says, and lets out a whistle as he turns around. "Not a bad place! Look at these paintings!" The walls are covered with gold-framed oil paintings of landscapes in different seasons. "We should have brought a wagon," he says, looking at Otto. "There is much to take here."

"It's too dangerous," Otto says. "Neighbors could see us pulling a wagon along the sidewalk. If we just walk out with our pockets bulging a little, no one will take any notice."

I have never seen a more luxurious room. The carpet is so deep it feels like I am standing on grass. Small crystals, glittering like little fish, dangle from the chandelier in the center of the ceiling. Dark green drapes cascade from rods held by brass hooks in the shape of horse heads above each window. Through the curtains falls just enough late afternoon light for us to see. Four stuffed wing chairs are arranged around a low oval table. Behind the glass doors of the sideboard I can make out a collection of beer steins and large tin cups with engravings. Several framed photographs on the mantel above the fireplace show members of the family next to portraits of the royal family. A tall young man with a high forehead and dark hair dressed in an officer's uniform. A wedding photograph. A small boy in a sailor's suit standing next to a toy sailboat. A young girl in a white dress with a large bow on her head sitting on a pony.

"Come on!" Otto calls. "It's not a museum! We should get out of here before it gets dark."

"Look at this. The Order of the Crown Cross, Third Class with Swords." I hold up the metal cross on a blue ribbon. "And here is a medal commemorating Kaiser Wilhelm I's hundredth birthday."

"I'm sure the man of the house is a hero," Robert says. "Let's go!"

"Didn't these people have to give up all their metal to support the war like the rest of us?" I ask. Plants are lined up next to the radiator, each of them growing out of a brass pot. My mind shifts to the time when we brought Mama's copper pan and water kettle to the resource collection agency. Oma and Mama had even exchanged their wedding rings for thin iron rings and a certificate that praised them for giving "gold for iron."

"The rich don't have to give up anything!" Otto snorts. "Wait until you see their pantry!"

We reach the kitchen at the end of a long hallway. The pantry is filled with sacks of flour, sugar, and lentils. Canned fruits and dried sausages are lined up on a shelf.

"How did they get all this?" I ask. Robert is already chewing on a piece of cheese he has taken from an earthen container.

"Don't you know that the rich are not suffering? They have connections and money. And they look out for their own," Otto says.

"That's what we're doing right now as well," Robert says. I still haven't gotten used to the stealing. But my mouth is watering from the aroma of the sausage and I take a bite. It's been a while since I tasted sausage. Next I grab the cheese and break it in half to share with Emil.

"Don't take more than fits easily into your pockets," Otto warns. "Remember! This is just a reconnaissance mission. We will come back when we can take more. Today we just walk away with a full stomach and this!" Otto opens a drawer in the kitchen cupboard and turns around, waving a bundle of bills. "My sister told me that this is where the cook keeps her grocery money."

"No!" I blurt out. "The cook will get in trouble if we take her money!"

The others all look at me. Robert's eyes shift to Otto, waiting for him to respond first. Otto frowns. "So you're suddenly growing a conscience?" he asks. "That's a bit late. We've broken into this villa and eaten their food.

Next time we'll come back for more. What's your problem?" He hands each of us five Marks. I shake my head.

"Suit yourself," he says, and shrugs. "That leaves more for us this time. But if you stick with us you'd better get over your scruples soon, since we'll return next weekend."

Outside, dusk has fallen, but the streetlights are not yet lit. We join the few pedestrians on the sidewalk. No one talks. I wish I could talk to Hans right now. How could he steal like this? But when he returns, the war will be over and there will be no need for more Operation Sundays. I know that I won't come back to the villa. There has to be another way to make the last five Marks I need to buy the sewing machine. I have at least one Mark's worth of cigarettes. Maybe Herr Goldmann will give me another assignment soon. Or maybe I will win the poetry contest. When we reach the Roland Fountain and there still are no police in sight I breathe easier.

thirteen

Hedwig has asked me to take her place in the queue at the butcher's so she can stand in line for milk. When I leave work it is already dark and a cold wind blows. I button up my jacket and bury my hands in my pockets. At the corner of Charlottenstrasse and Auguststrasse I see a group of people standing on the curb under the streetlight. I stop and push myself into the crowd to see what they are looking at. A dead horse lies on the cobblestones, or rather its remains. The head is still intact, but the carcass has been butchered, releasing the strong smell of raw meat. The horse's intestines are spilled out on the street like a giant earthworm.

"What happened?" I ask a boy next to me.

"It collapsed and fell down. The old man tried to get it back on its feet to continue pulling the carriage, but it just made this terrible sound, and closed its eyes," the boy says. "And now they are cutting it up."

A woman stands next to the carcass with a large knife. The yellow light of the street lamp reflects on the blade before she cuts into a shoulder. She has rolled up the sleeves of her coat and her arms and hands are bloody. It starts to drizzle and then the rain comes down in a cold steady mist.

An old man is staring at the scene. His cheeks are glistening and I cannot tell if they are wet from rain or if he is crying.

"Is he the one who drove the cart?" I ask the boy.

"Yes." He nods. "I helped him to pull the gear off the horse."

"Are you going to get a piece of horsemeat?" I ask the boy.

"I hope so," he says. "My mother has the Spanish flu and we haven't had any meat for two weeks."

The rain gets stronger and I step back onto the sidewalk to make way for the blood that washes down toward the sewer. The woman with the knife hands the next slab of meat to an old woman in the front row. She wraps the meat in a piece of brown paper and hurries down the sidewalk. The people who are still waiting for meat have now formed a short queue. The boy motions me to come closer. "Come over here. You can be with me in line."

"No. Thank you!" I say. I remember the horrible smell of cooked horsemeat. Hedwig has ration cards for pork and I will pick it up at the butcher's.

Hedwig greets me with an annoyed look when I get to the butcher at Louisenstrasse. "There you are, finally," she says. "I hope Oma hasn't jumped out the window by now. We can't leave her alone for such long periods anymore."

"I don't think she would jump out the window," I say. "Remember, she doesn't like fresh air." Hedwig doesn't even respond, just hands me the ration cards. "We really need to get meat. See you later at home."

There are about fifteen people in front of me, most of them women, some with small children. A little girl, standing with the woman behind me, turns to her mother and asks, "When will we get food?"

"Soon," the mother says. "We'll make ourselves a nice soup. That will make us warm inside."

"I'm hungry now," the little girl whines.

"I know, darling," the mother tries to soothe her. "But we have to wait here until we get the meat."

"Let's hope there is some left by the time our turn comes," a stout woman in front of me chimes in. "Yesterday, I stood in line at the bakery for three hours, just to learn that they were out of bread when I reached the front of the line."

"Yes," the girl's mother says. "That happened to my older daughter the other day, too."

"I heard that the Poles take all the food that is meant for Berlin and keep it for themselves. It doesn't even reach the outskirts of the city. They have these gangs of highwaymen that waylay the food transports," the stout woman says.

"What's going on now?" someone asks. There is a commotion ahead of us.

"No, no, no!" a woman screams, and pounds her fist against the shop window. Her brown cape falls from her shoulders and when she turns around to pick it up I notice the same green sheen on her hair that Mama has as a result of her work in the ammunition factory. "This can't be! I've waited here for six hours. I have ration cards for meat. Give it to me now!"

Other women also begin to pound against the window. The butcher appears in the doorway, but withdraws quickly once he sees the wall of women closing in on him. I hear the door slam shut.

"Oh, no!" The mother turns to the little girl.

"What happened, Mami?"

"They are out of meat," the mother says.

The queue dissolves and some of the women walk away with hunched shoulders, shaking their heads. I step aside and watch the remaining women congregate in a circle in front of the butcher shop. The woman in the brown cape calls out, "I've had enough of this now! Let's go to the Food Administration!" The other women respond with clapping and loud murmurs. The women talk briefly and soon after head briskly down the road. There might be a story here. I am in no hurry to get home, where yet another dinner of bad bread with turnip jam or thin milk soup is waiting for me. So I decide to follow them.

The office of the Berlin Food Rationing Administration

is nearby. I stay close to the group as they storm inside. A secretary tries to keep them from going any farther and asks whom they wish to speak to, but the stout woman pushes her aside, calling out, "We need to see the director!" She opens the door to the next room, where a white-haired man sits behind a desk.

"Who are you?" He looks up, startled, a monocle squeezed in his right eye.

"We are Berliner housewives and children who need food!" the woman says, and steps toward his desk.

"I am sorry," the man says, slowly getting up from his chair. "We do not distribute food here." A sizable belly bulges from under his vest.

"What do you distribute?" another woman asks.

"Hunger? Poverty? Illness?" the stout woman suggests.

"I am very sorry," the old man says again, "but I have to ask you to leave."

"Look at this." The mother with the child picks up a sandwich from the man's desk. "Apparently, you have no trouble finding food for yourself!" She smells the bread and calls out, "This is real bread with cold cuts! How dare you eat like this while we are standing outside the butcher's for naught?"

"Fräulein Meier, please call the police!" The old man is trying to make eye contact with his secretary, but the doorway is blocked by the women. I am pressing my back against the warm tile oven, enjoying the heat seeping through my jacket.

"Ladies," the man addresses the women. "I told you. We print and distribute the ration cards, but we don't have any food for you."

"Just food for yourselves!" The woman in the cape shakes her head. "We don't want to starve any longer!" she says loudly. Several other women echo her demand.

"End this war and give us bread!" another woman calls out. Through the window I see the police arrive. The men in uniform swiftly come inside. "Please leave Dr. Müller's office!" they demand. "Otherwise we will have to take you into custody!"

"Take us into custody for what? For hunger? For wanting to feed our children?" the woman in the cape asks. But the other women are ready to leave and file through the main door back onto the sidewalk. Soon the group disperses. As I walk toward the subway station I can't get the image of the little girl eyeing the man's sandwich out of my head. In my mind I begin to compose an article that I will write once I reach home. "Berliner Housewives Demand Food: Director of Food Administration Eats Cold-Cut Sandwiches While Little Girl Is Starving."

fourteen

This is very well written, Moritz," Herr Goldmann says when I deliver the article to his office the next day during my lunch break. "You have a good sense for interesting stories and strike the right balance so we shouldn't have any problems with the censor. We'll run it later today. If I can get it on the front page, you'll get paid double." I'm glad to hear a compliment about my writing but I am even happier about the double pay since I just saw the names of the winners of the war bond poetry contest published in the paper. I did not win.

"How did you happen to be there?" he asks.

"I was standing in line for meat when the butcher ran out of stock, and the women decided to storm the Food Administration office. It was so sad to see the little girl hungry while the fat director ate a sandwich in front of her," I say.

"Some people have everything while others are starving," Herr Goldmann says. I nod, remembering what I saw in the villa. "More and more people are fed up with the ersatz food, the war, the injustice, and all that misery." He shakes his head. "But isn't your mother Anna Schmidt? I just learned that recently. You should have told me."

"Yes, she's my mother," I say. "And she has to hide from the police because they would arrest her for her speeches since she expresses a 'treasonable opinion.'"

"That's what they call speaking the truth nowadays," Herr Goldmann says.

"Are you a social democrat as well?" I ask.

"I'm not a member of any party, but I most certainly will vote, when we finally have free elections," he says. "Thanks to men and women like your mother we will have a democratic Germany. You must be proud of her."

"But it is treason to speak out against the Kaiser and the war," I say, thinking of the policeman waiting for her in front of our house.

"You cannot honestly defend the Kaiser and his military hubris or an election system that represents people according to their class and wealth?"

"You sound just like my mother," I say.

"Yes, I hope I do. But the difference is that I'm saying this only to you, when we are alone. She is calling out in back rooms and on street corners," he says. "That's what I call courage!"

I look out of the window, thinking about what Herr

Goldmann has just said. *You should be proud of your mother.* I never thought of it that way.

"Have you had lunch yet?" Herr Goldmann asks.

"No," I say. "I wanted to bring you the article first."

"Let me buy you lunch at the Golden Goose," he says, and grabs his jacket.

The Golden Goose is jam-packed and Herr Goldmann looks for an empty table. A man waves in the corner and Herr Goldmann motions for me to follow him.

"How are you, Aaron?" the man asks, and points to the two empty chairs at his table. "Sit down and eat with me. I haven't ordered yet."

Herr Goldmann sits down, stretching his stiff leg out to the side of his chair, and pulls out the other chair for me.

"Kurt," he says, "this is Moritz Schmidt, one of our printers, but also a talented young writer who I am trying to groom as a journalist. He just wrote a great piece about the distribution of food in favor of the rich."

I shake the strong hand the man holds out to me. He seems a little older than Herr Goldmann, with a high forehead and a black mustache.

"Nice to meet you," he says.

"Moritz," Herr Goldmann says, "Kurt Berg is one of the most talented writers I know. He's back from the Eastern Front, where he successfully escaped the Russian wrath to the benefit of readers in this town."

"Yeah, yeah, you old sweet-talker," Herr Berg says with a dismissive gesture.

"And wasn't it your name I read today as the winner

of the poetry contest for the ninth war bond?" Herr Goldmann asks. "I think your poem was called 'In Spite of It All.' Congratulations!"

Herr Berg laughs and says, "Thank you! Must have been a weak field of contenders." I avert my eyes, thinking I was part of it.

"With your prize money you should buy us lunch," Herr Goldmann says, and turns around to call for the waitress. A blond girl, her apron tightly wrapped around her waist, comes to take the order. When she greets us Herr Berg and Herr Goldmann exchange knowing glances. "What would you like, gentlemen?" the waitress asks. Blue eyes twinkling, she's obviously enjoying the men's admiring looks.

"We'd like three pork roasts with dumplings and red cabbage," Herr Berg says, smiling.

"We only have what's written on that board over there," she says. "Haven't served pork roast since 1917."

The men laugh and order three bowls of soup and coffee. After the waitress has left, Herr Berg sighs and looks after her. "Oh, the beauty of the female of the species."

"She's a pretty girl, but too young for you," Herr Goldmann says. "Maybe Moritz would like her."

I try to think of something witty to say but my brain is frozen.

"No, I'm not interested," I say instead, causing the two of them to smile.

"Not yet, maybe," Herr Berg says, and I hope they will change the topic of conversation before I blush again.

The waitress brings our soup and I listen to the men's conversation. I learn that Herr Berg worked in an office at the Eastern Front as a censor for letters. He talks about the boredom of the daily task but also of the despair and hopelessness many soldiers expressed in their letters. Maybe that's why Hans never writes to me about Mama's political activities or details about the war. My own comments about Mama might have been blacked out as well. I knew that correspondence was censored, but had never thought about what that really meant for my family.

The waitress brings the bill and we leave. On the way back to the printshop I think about the time I saw Hans kissing Erma Klinger. They were standing in the corner of our backyard one night when I came home from work. She had her arms around his waist while his hands were hidden inside her blouse. I stood for a moment watching them in their embrace before I climbed up the stairs to our apartment. Later, when Hans came to the bedroom, I asked him how it felt to kiss a girl. "There is nothing to compare it with," he said. But I begged him to try a description. "You know when the barber has shaved the nape of your neck and then goes over that spot with that thick soft brush to wipe away the little hairs?"

"That just tickles," I said.

"Imagine that kind of tickle all over your body," Hans said, and pulled the cover over his head. That was two weeks before he left for the war.

fifteen

The sewing machine is still there when I reach the pawnshop after work. Its price is unchanged, and with the four Marks I received for the article about the events at the Food Administration I have enough. I watch the fat man count the bills with his pudgy fingers. Back on the street I motion a horse carriage to stop.

"What you got there, boy?" the old man who holds the reins asks.

"It's a sewing machine," I say, wishing that I had brought an umbrella as the rain now whips my face.

"Alfred can help you," the old man says, and motions to a boy who sits huddled in a blanket on the backseat. When the boy pushes himself off the carriage I can see that he won't be much help. He cannot be more than ten years old, and he looks gaunt and skinny.

"Alfred, help to lift the machine into the back," the

old man calls. Alfred tries to push, but his bony wrists begin to tremble as soon as he strains his arms, and I gently motion him to step aside. Once the machine is in the back of the carriage, Alfred wraps the blanket around it before we both sit down on the backseat.

"He's a little skinny, my grandson," the old man says when he lifts the reins and the horse begins to pull. "But he needs to help out. His sisters both have rickets. They don't even grow anymore. Their mother's down with the flu. Father's in a prison camp in France."

We pass a butcher shop where a policeman guards the line of women and children on the sidewalk.

"Here they have to protect the butchers from their own customers, but in Russia they have food for everyone every day. Their revolution brought peace and food. It's about time we follow suit here."

I look at Alfred, who shivers. "Do you have a fever?" I whisper.

"No," he says quietly. "I'm just always cold."

The rain has stopped and I take the blanket off the machine to wrap it back around his shoulders.

"What can you do with that machine? Does it make food?" the old man asks.

"No," I say. "My mother used to sew coats and aprons for a living."

"Seems like nowadays everyone is trading goods for food or coal. You must be lucky that you can use your money for a sewing machine."

"We need my mother to work from home," I say.

"For the money you paid for this machine you could have bought meat and real anthracite coal briquettes, not the soft stuff they hand out on ration cards," the old man says, and shakes his head.

When we stop in front of Aunt Martha's house I pay the driver, and he orders Alfred to help me carry the machine upstairs. We move slowly and have to stop for Alfred to shake out his arms after every flight. Once we reach Aunt Martha's apartment on the fourth floor he leans against the wall, breathing heavily.

"Are you all right?" I ask.

"Yes," he sighs. "Is this where you live?"

"No," I say. "This is my aunt's place, but my mother stays here right now. That's why I've brought the machine up here."

He nods and then asks, "What's your favorite food?"

"My favorite food?"

"Yes," he says. "What kind of food do you think about before you go to sleep? It's a game I play with my sisters."

"I like real bread and I like fried sausage," I say, looking at him skeptically. "But I don't think it's a good idea to think too much about food if you're hungry." Maybe he does have a fever after all.

"Pot roast and gravy are my favorites, and dumplings, nice and sticky, with steam coming out when you tear them apart with your fork," he says.

"Those are nice, too," I say. "But right now nobody eats them."

"I think of food all the time," he says, and I worry that he will start to cry.

"Do you want to come inside and warm up? I'm sure my aunt has a warm kitchen."

"No, no. I should get back down to Grandpa," Alfred says, and begins to walk down the stairs. I wish I had something edible to give him.

Aunt Martha opens the door when I knock.

"Is Mama here yet?" I ask.

"No," she says. "But she should come any minute."

Aunt Martha looks at the sewing machine. "I don't know how to sew, my boy."

"It's for Mama," I say, and when she steps aside I push the machine across the parquet in the hallway to the living room. She follows me, each of her steps a hard click on the wooden floor.

"How old are you?" she asks.

"Sixteen," I say, trying to read in her stern face where she is going with this.

"Sixteen," she repeats. "A boy of sixteen should know better."

"Better than what?"

"Better than wasting his money. Money your family could use for food," she says, and turns around. I take a breath to defend myself, but her shoes are already clicking on the parquet in the hallway and next I hear the sound of the hanger bouncing back after she has taken her coat.

"Are you going out?" I ask, still standing next to the sewing machine in the living room.

"Yes," she says, fastening her hat. "I'll see you later."

Soon after, I hear a key in the door, and when Mama enters the living room I quickly step next to the sewing machine and point to it with my right arm stretched out.

"Look what I got for you!" I call.

"Oh, Moritz!" Mama says. "How did you get the money to buy it back?" She gives me a stern look.

"I saved it for a long time. I've been writing a few articles for the paper," I say, searching her face for the joy I expected to see.

"I hope you didn't get involved in any crooked business, like your brother used to be," she says, and I let my arm sink.

"We could have used the money to buy food," she says.

"I thought you could sew again."

"Moritz, it was a very nice thought. I might start sewing again one day. But I won't sit down to assemble army coats for eighty-five pfennig apiece."

"But that's what you used to do."

"That's what I used to do when your father earned money, your little sister was alive, and you were a little boy."

"It's not that long ago. If you earned money from sewing you wouldn't have to work in an ammunition factory or on a construction site. Everything could be the way it used to be."

"During the war women have had to work in these industries, Moritz. It was not my choice. But it turns out that in addition to earning a living I can convince other workingmen and women to go out on the streets to fight for their rights and to help us end this war."

She steps toward me, her arms open, but I press my back against the wall. I don't want her to touch me.

"You're right." Mama smiles and lets her arms fall against her skirt. "You are too old for a hug, aren't you, now?"

I don't feel too old for anything. For a moment, I want to throw myself onto the floor and pound my fists against the carpet until Mama sits down at the sewing machine. But instead I watch her walk into the kitchen, where she opens the lid over the stove to stoke the fire. When I turn toward the sewing machine I see my own reflection in the windowpane, the reflection of a boy who should have known better.

sixteen

The letter has a postage stamp from the Army Mail in Metz on the top right corner and is addressed to Family Schmidt. I don't recognize the handwriting on the envelope, but it must be from Hans since he is stationed near Metz. Do they address death notices to the entire family? Wasn't there an official seal on the letter that told us when Papa had died? My heart races as I walk up to Aunt Martha's apartment holding the envelope between my thumb and index finger as if it could explode when pressed too hard.

Mama opens the door after I knock three times.

"Moritz!" she says. "But Hedwig is already here. Are you sure no one followed you?"

"Don't worry!" After a full week of guarding the main entrance of our house, the pig-faced policeman stopped coming. Mama said that they found more important people to hunt for, but Aunt Martha thinks that it is not safe enough for her to go back home. As we make our way into the kitchen I notice a limp in Mama's gait. "What happened to you?"

"Oh, I'm a little clumsy with the bricks and let one load drop onto my foot," she says. The image of Mama carrying heavy loads of bricks on a construction site sends a flash of anger through me and the words leave my mouth before I think: "If you hadn't gotten involved with politics you wouldn't have to do this hard work."

"Moritz, my dear." She turns to me. "I wish you'd understand that I don't do this to spite you. I'm a social democrat because it is time for us to end this war and fight for a better life for people like us."

We reach the kitchen, where Hedwig is preparing dinner, cutting up turnips and wrinkled potatoes.

"A letter came," I say.

A shadow falls over Mama's eyes and she asks, "A letter from Hans?"

I hand it to her and say, "I don't recognize the handwriting, but it is postmarked in Metz so it must be from Hans."

Mama slices the envelope open with a knife and begins to read.

Dear Family Schmidt,

I am writing to you from the field hospital in Ors near Metz. My name is Ursula Wegner and I am a nurse here. Hans Schmidt has been badly injured in a battle against the enemy. Hans Schmidt is a brave man and defended our Fatherland with courage. He is currently unable to write to you personally, but he wants you all to know how much he loves you and misses you. If you would like to write to him he would greatly appreciate it and his recovery could only benefit from a few words from the ones who love him. Please send any correspondence for him c/o Ursula Wegner at the Field Hospital in Ors near Metz, Reichsland Alsace-Lorraine. I will be happy to read your letters to him.

Regards,
Ursula Wegner

"What does this mean?" Hedwig asks.

"It means he is so badly injured that he can neither write nor read by himself," I say. I take the letter from Mama's hand and reread the nurse's precise cursive.

seventeen

For the next two days everything inside of me hurts. I don't tell anyone at work about Hans's letter. I take the back exit after work to avoid meeting Herr Goldmann. But he catches me on the way to the subway. "Hello, stranger! I haven't seen you in a while. How are you?"

"I'm fine. Thank you."

"Why don't I believe you? You look like three days of rain. What's the matter?"

"Nothing."

"You can't fool me, old friend."

"We've got a letter from my brother. He's in a hospital near Metz, badly injured."

"I am sorry," Herr Goldmann says. "How bad are the injuries?"

"A nurse wrote the letter. She says that he can't write himself and that he can't read." I have to swallow. "I don't know exactly what is wrong with him. But if he can't write it must be bad. He is a watchmaker, he needs his hand . . ."

"Oh my God!" Herr Goldmann says, and bends forward to embrace me. I don't step back but let myself sink into his arms. My tears are soaked up by the coarse wool of his jacket. His hug feels good and he offers me his handkerchief to blow my nose. The cotton smells like tobacco.

"I would invite you to a good meal at the Goose, but I am afraid it is one of these meatless days in the city, and I don't think I could cheer you up with turnip patties and fried war bread."

"Thank you," I say, and even manage to smile. "But I'm not hungry anyway and I have to get home."

"I understand," he says. "Maybe soon you'd like to take another writing job?"

"Sure," I say.

<hr>

At home, Hedwig and I take turns attending to Oma. We don't mention the letter to her. We hardly talk at all. Days pass between working in the printshop, standing in line for rationed food, and visiting Mama. Friday evening I sit on my bed and try to write a letter to Hans. But what can I possibly say to him or to Miss Wegner, who will read my words to him? Soon a small mound of crumpled paper piles up on my pillow and I give up. I pull the cigar box out from under my bed and unfold his previous letters, those written by his own hand, but reading them hurts too much.

I lie awake for a long time, thinking about Hans and trying not to think about him. When I finally doze off I see Hans stepping out of a train, pausing on the platform. His uniform is dirty, and as he slowly turns around his right arm falls off and lands on the platform, bleeding. I run toward Hans, but his face shows no sign that he recognizes me. Standing in front of him, calling his name, I notice the same smell of blood I remember from the horse's carcass. When I look up I see that where Hans's eyes used to be his face shows two hollow cavities. He opens his mouth to speak but I can't hear any words.

I wake up from the nightmare all sweaty, and for a while I leave the light on for fear I will fall back into the same dream. After a restless night, I get up early and try to forget the dream by carrying the little remaining coal we have left from the basement to the kitchen. The weather has turned colder and soon we will have to find new heating fuel. I light the fire in the tile oven and heat up some water for tea. It is still dark outside. I warm my hands on the enamel cup with the steaming tea, think of Hans, and wonder what it looks like where he is now. How lonely he must be. The more I think about Hans the more certain I become. I need to see him!

When I reach work in the morning I complain about a headache and cough loudly.

"What's the matter with you?" Old Moser says as he begins to set the type for the midday edition.

"I am not feeling so good," I say, holding my head.

"Hope you don't have that Spanish flu, boy," Old Moser says.

"Better send him home before he coughs it all over us," Mahlke says.

"Want to go home, boy?" Old Moser looks at me, his forehead in a frown.

"Maybe I'd better," I mumble, trying to avoid direct eye contact. I'm a bad liar.

"Go see a doctor," Mahlke says. "We don't want you to die on us!"

"Don't come back before you're well again," Old Moser calls after me. "We can handle this shop for a few days."

I nod and lift my hand in a weak farewell before I leave the printshop. This was easier than I thought.

eighteen

The train to Metz leaves Zoo station only twenty minutes after I get there, just enough time to buy a newspaper. While I am waiting for the train I skim the front page. Ludendorff has resigned.

The third-class compartment fills quickly, but I find a window seat on a bench close to the door. Across from me sits a girl, reading a book. Two women stop in the aisle and push their bags under my bench. The older, broader one squeezes herself next to me, while the slimmer woman takes a seat next to the girl on the opposite bench.

Soon after, the engine lets out a high-pitched whistle and the train sets in motion. The two women talk loudly about their visit to Berlin and how much they are looking forward to returning to Kassel.

"No wonder the Kaiser prefers his castle in

Wilhelmshöhe to staying in Berlin. What a terrible monster of a city," the younger one complains.

"So dirty!" the other comments.

"I've heard that people saw the Kaiser walking in Tiergarten, all broken and sad-looking."

"How brave of him to even show himself in public. I'm sure that among the socialists are some who'd like to kill him."

"Poor Wilhelm II." The woman next to me shakes her head. "How dare this American Wilson demand he abdicate."

"But this won't happen, since the Reich will win this war," the younger one says, to which they both nod and then look down at their hands.

For a while, I hear only the rhythmic chugging of the train. When I turn my head away from the window, both women are asleep, their chins resting on their scarves. The girl is still reading, her head bobbing with each sway of the train. She doesn't look up, just turns the page once in a while, engrossed in her book.

As the train clatters onward, hours later I watch the flat landscape on the other side of the window slowly growing dark. I pull my jacket tighter around me and lean my head against the backrest, dozing, dreaming of the printshop.

I wake up shivering and rub my eyes with icy fingers. The train is not heated. The girl still sits across from me, reading her book by the dim light. The two women have

left the train and we are now alone on the two benches, facing each other. On the other side of the aisle a mother and her son are wrapped in a blanket, both sleeping. The train slows as it enters the Trier train station. I must have slept a long time. When we stop I step toward the exit to look for a place to buy a hot beverage, but the station-master already blows the whistle and raises his signal. The engine lets out a loud sigh and steam billows as the train pulls out of the station. A few new passengers find their seats and I walk back and forth along the swaying aisle, trying to get warm. When I sit down again the girl sitting on the opposite seat looks at me.

"Would you like some tea?" she says, and pulls a thermos from a basket next to her feet.

"Thank you." My hands shake as I take the small cup with the steaming liquid.

"It's cold in here," she says. She must be about my age. Her white, translucent skin makes her look fragile. Faint freckles spread over her nose and cheeks. Above a high forehead her black hair is parted in the middle and two thick plaits are tucked in half circles around her head, like a braided halo.

"Yes, I had forgotten that they don't heat trains anymore," I say.

"I hope we don't have another winter like last year ahead of us. With the Spanish flu and not enough heating fuel it will be gruesome," she says. I nod and think about my little sister, Louise.

"Where are you going?" the girl asks, taking out a second enamel cup from her basket to pour herself some tea. I notice how slim her hands are, with long thin fingers, like a porcelain puppet's.

"To Metz," I say, almost scalding my lips with the hot tea. "How about you?"

"I'm just going to visit my aunt who lives on the Moselle River for two days," she says. "My name is Rebecca."

"Moritz." I lift my cap and nod. "What are you reading?"

"Karl May."

"Oh." I'm surprised. His work is mostly about cowboys and Indians, not really the kind of book I thought a girl might like. "Which book?"

"The last of the Winnetou series. Do you know Karl May?"

"Yes," I say. "I used to read him but I haven't read the latest Winnetou."

"It's good, but different from the others in the series. This is the only book Karl May wrote after he actually had visited America. Isn't it great that he could imagine all these Indian and cowboy stories without ever having set foot on American soil?"

"I guess so," I say. "But I don't really think America is so great."

"That's not what I am saying. All I am saying is that Karl May is a good writer."

"Yes, he is good, but I don't really want to read anything right now that takes place in America. After all, America supports the enemy." As soon as I have said this

I wish I could take it back. Her nose and upper lip pull together in a mock frown that gives her a comical look. Suddenly she doesn't look so fragile anymore.

"Oh, you think I am supporting the enemy by reading a book set in America. I'm weakening the war effort?" Now her eyebrows are raised and she smiles, two small dimples forming on each of her cheeks.

"I'm just saying—" I start, but she doesn't let me finish.

"Karl May went to America in 1908. He died before the war began. I don't think we can blame him for conspiring with the enemy." She speaks so loudly that the mother and her son are startled awake and turn their heads in our direction. But Rebecca is unfazed. Her dark, bold eyes seem to enjoy this argument. I don't even know how our conversation arrived at this point.

"Thank you for the tea." I return the cup after I wipe it out with my handkerchief.

"You're welcome," she says, and wraps the thermos with the cups in a towel before she places them back in the basket. The train slows down and Rebecca gets up. "This is my stop," she says. "Nice meeting you."

"You forgot your book," I call after her.

"I finished it. You can keep it for your return trip," she says, and before she turns around to walk toward the exit she adds, "Read it if you dare!"

nineteen

It is dark when the train reaches Metz. The arrival hall with its vaulted ceiling looks more like a cathedral than a train station. Arched windows on the high walls are decorated with scenes from German myths in stained glass. Friezes, adorned with intricate figures and detailed scenes chiseled from stone, spread out between pillars. As I look for an exit sign, a boy, maybe ten or eleven years old, smiles at me and says, "Welcome to Metz! The capital of the Reichsland Alsace-Lorraine and the Kaiser's favorite city!" I nod and try to pass him, but he steps in my way.

"Would you like me to give you a tour? Let me show you the Kaiser's lounge." I shake my head. The boy is dressed in a threadbare brown felt jacket, several sizes too big for him. He continues to smile at me, pushing the rim of his cap from his forehead, unperturbed by my lack of interest. "This station was opened in 1908. It sits on 3,000 steel pillars, some of them almost 56 feet deep in the earth. The platforms are extra-broad to accommodate movement of troops on horseback and large military equipment to and from the trains." I walk on but I don't seem to be able to shake him off. "Metz also has a cathedral and several forts on the outskirts of the city."

"Listen! Do I look like I want a tour? It is eight-thirty in the evening. I just got here after a twelve-hour train ride. What do you want from me?"

"I want to give you a tour."

"How much do you charge for the tour?"

"Two Marks."

"I'll give you one Mark if you just leave me alone."

He considers this. "I could give you a short tour, just the station and the old part of town."

"My friend, it is raining. I'm cold and hungry. I need to find a place to sleep for the night. Please take the Mark and leave me alone!"

"I can show you a place to stay. It's cheap and clean."

"Where is that?"

"It's a short walk from here."

"All right. I'll give you two Marks and you'll bring me to this hotel."

"It's not really a hotel. It's more like a private accommodation," he says as we cross the square in front of the train station.

"How much will they charge?"

"Five Marks for the night. Fifty pfennig for a meal," he

says before he stops again to point to a statue on the corner of the station building.

"You see Roland with his sword. The Kaiser insisted on it."

I turn around and nod. It is quite a massive building. The square in front of the station is filled with military vehicles and soldiers. A group of orderlies transports wounded men on stretchers, lining them up in front of the entrance to the third-class waiting room. An officer in riding pants and long black boots leads a horse out of a trailer.

"The stone was transported from Lorraine quarries and the clock tower was designed by the Kaiser himself. The stained-glass panels show—"

"Enough, enough! No more!" I hold up my right hand. "Tell me something about yourself. I'm Moritz. What's your name?"

"Karl or Charles," the boy says. "My father speaks French."

"Is he in the army?"

"Yes, he was."

"Where was he stationed?"

"They sent the bilingual soldiers from the Alsace-Lorraine to the Eastern Front for fear they would fraternize with the French soldiers."

"Did he come back?"

"Yes," Karl says. "He's home."

The rain has stopped but the air is so cold that we are walking fast to keep warm.

Only every third street lamp throws a beam on the sidewalk, but I can see that we are walking through a residential street lined on both sides with narrow three-story houses. The shingles here are flat and black, not rounded and made from red clay like the ones in Berlin. Next, we pass a field that has recently been harvested, and soon we enter a village where low, half-timbered houses sit behind hedges.

"What brings you to Metz?" Karl asks.

"I'm looking for my brother. He's in a field hospital in Ors."

"You can walk there from our house," Karl says.

"How close is the front?" I ask.

"Very close. You can hear the shelling on most days."

Karl stops in front of a small pub. "Could you give me the money now?" he asks. "I have to buy something here."

I give him the two coins and he quickly returns with a bottle neck sticking out of his pocket. We continue to walk, and as I am about to ask how much farther we'll have to go he stops and opens a low gate that leads into a small vegetable garden.

"Here we are," he says. Behind a low hedge stands a small half-timbered house. The dark brown logs meet at crooked angles, and with the rosebush growing next to the door it reminds me of a cottage from a fairy tale.

"Don't be scared of the dog!" Karl says, but the sight of a large black dog crossing the path in huge leaps already freezes me.

"Mietzi," Karl calls. "Come here!"

But Mietzi is already on her hind legs licking my face. I try to push her aside, but she jumps up again and snaps at my sleeve.

"She's just playing!" Karl says. "Look how she wags her tail. She's happy to see you."

I'm happy when Karl opens the front door and tells the dog to stay outside. I step over the wooden threshold into a cold room. Two oil lamps flicker from a sideboard and three candles stuck into empty bottles on a table provide dim light.

"There you are, Karl." A girl, younger than Karl, comes running toward us and stops when she sees me. "Oh, you brought someone."

"This is Moritz from Berlin. He'll stay the night with us," Karl explains.

"Good evening," I say, and shake her ice-cold hand.

"Why did you let the fire go out, Marie?"

"Papa wouldn't let me go outside. He yelled every time I came near the door."

"Go quickly now and make the fire. We need to eat."

"Karl!" A man's voice comes from behind a curtain.

"Papa," Karl says. "How are you?"

"Same as always," Karl's father barks. "Did you bring me the schnapps?" Karl walks over, pulls the curtain aside, and hands his father the bottle. "Here," he says. "And this is Moritz. He'll stay for the night."

"Mhhhh." The man puts the bottle to his mouth and drinks hastily. "Ahhhhhh!" he sighs, placing the bottle on his bed stand. I now notice that he has only one arm.

"Yes, Herr Moritz, this is what happens when you fight for Kaiser and fatherland. I'm left with one arm and I also lost my right foot." He stretches his right leg out from under the cover. A bandage covers the stump.

"Moritz is looking for his brother. He's in the field hospital in Ors."

"Hope it's just a minor injury. Depending how bad it hits you, one is better off dead," Karl's father says.

Marie has made the fire and stirs a pot on the stove with a wooden spoon. The room slowly warms up. "Where is your mother?" I ask.

"She died three months ago from the flu," Karl says.

"I'm sorry," I say.

"Don't be sorry, Herr Moritz. She got out before she had to live with a cripple," Karl's father bellows from his bed. Without turning around I can hear him take another swig from the bottle.

Marie serves us each a bowl of oatmeal with thick, creamy milk. "Where do you get the milk?" I ask.

"We have a cow in the backyard. We can grow enough grass and grain to feed her and then we trade the milk for sausage from the butcher," Karl explains.

"And Mietzi gets the scraps because the butcher's wife likes her," Marie adds.

"Do you go to school?" I ask.

"Not right now," Karl explains. "Our school has been closed. The teacher has been drafted and they couldn't find a willing replacement to come this close to the front."

I search for words, but I cannot come up with any

more conversation. We finish our meal in silence. When I help clear the dishes I see Karl's father now snoring loudly next to the empty bottle.

"The biggest expense we have is the schnapps for Papa," Karl explains. "That's why I have to earn extra money as a tour guide or by taking people in for the night."

"If he doesn't have the schnapps he has bad dreams and talks with people who aren't in the room," Marie adds as she hands me a set of clean linens.

"We have an extra bed in here," Karl says, and opens the door to the back room.

I lie awake for a long time, listening to the rain outside, thinking about this sad little family. Before I fall asleep I decide that in the morning I will leave more money than they were asking for the bed and the meal.

twenty

I leave the house before Karl and Marie are up. It is still dark outside and dense fog lies heavy on the village. Before we went to bed Karl had pointed to a path behind their house, leading from their garden to the river. The damp cold seeps into the fabric of my jacket and I pull it tighter around me. Once I reach the Moselle I continue on an elevated gravel path from where I can hear the river next to me. When I reach the village of Ors, the fog has lifted and bright sunshine illuminates the low hill on the other side of the river covered in the red, yellow, and orange patchwork colors of a forest in autumn. On this side of the Moselle rows of woody vines grow on sloped fields. I pass an old woman in a long woolen dress picking off clusters of grapes. I don't have to ask my way, for I see a military truck with a large red cross painted on its side doors parked in front of a two-story building. Two orderlies are lifting a soldier from the back of the truck onto a stretcher. This must have been a school once, as wooden chairs and ink-stained desks are stored under a roof to the right side of the yard. The sharp stench of disinfectant mixed with the odor of dirty clothing fills the building. I pass through a corridor where a nurse pushes a squeaking cart with bedpans. "I'm looking for a patient, Hans Schmidt," I tell her, and she points to the room at the end of the corridor where an older nurse sits behind a desk, writing on the outside of a folder. I repeat my question; she confirms the spelling and tells me to go upstairs to find Ward 2.

"Can I help you?" A tall nurse appears when I enter the room. A white starched cap with a red cross sits on her head like a tiara.

"I'm looking for Hans Schmidt," I say.

"He's over here." She points to the bed next to the door. "But it's hard to recognize him."

I stare at the man in the bed, trying to find a familiar feature, anything that shows this is my brother's face. His forehead and eyes are covered with a bandage. His right cheek looks like a boiled cabbage leaf framed by a thick pink scar that runs into his upper lip.

"What happened to his face?" I whisper.

"He was too close to a gas explosion," the nurse says, motioning for me to come closer.

But I can't move. "Are you sure this is him?" I whisper.

"Yes, we are," the nurse says. "He carried his papers

when they brought him in and he talked just before they operated on him."

She straightens the blanket and I notice the hollow below his right shoulder.

"What happened to his arm?"

"He lost half of his right arm," she says, and lifts the blanket for a moment so I can see the stump, wrapped in white gauze.

"Are you Frau Wegner?"

She nods.

"Thank you for your letter," I say without taking my eyes off Hans.

"Good morning, Hans. You have a visitor," she says.

Hans nods slightly and moves his lips.

"I can't hear him," I say, now standing closer. On the bed stand I notice his watch, the lid open and twisted, under the shattered glass a gash between the two hands, frozen at ten minutes after eight.

"It's hard for him to talk. He's still in shock and suffers a lot of pain. The morphine makes him very drowsy on top of that."

"Hans, it's me, Moritz," I say.

He opens his mouth but only a deep groan leaves his lips, followed by a slim rivulet of saliva running down his chin.

I sit down on the side of the bed and place my hand in his. After the nurse leaves we stay like this, motionless, for what seems like a very long time.

twenty-one

The tower of the Kaiser Wilhelm Memorial Church looms in the distance, faintly outlined by the dim orange light from the few working street lamps on Kurfürstendamm. After the long ride in an unheated train my legs feel frozen, and I move stiffly to the stairs leading to the subway station. While waiting for the train I pace up and down the platform. Pola Negri, the famous actress, looks down from an exotic movie poster on the billboard next to the ticket counter, reminding me how much Hans loves watching films. I hope that after his left eye recovers he can still enjoy them.

A loud rattle from inside the tunnel announces the arrival of the subway. I sit down next to a woman with a pram filled with firewood. The air in the compartment smells used and damp. When I leave the subway I take two stairs at once and hurry down the three blocks to our house, hoping that Hedwig has found enough heating fuel to warm at least one room. My fingers are still cold when I dig in my pockets for the key to the house door.

"Look who's here!" Otto suddenly appears out of the dark, putting his arm around my shoulders. I am so startled that I drop the keys.

"What are you doing here? I thought we only met on Sundays," I say, trying to wriggle away from Otto's grasp.

"Did you think we'd forget about you?" Robert bends down close to my face.

"What do you want?" I ask.

"What do *we* want?" Otto looks at Robert. "We want you to pay for what you did."

"I didn't do anything," I say.

"You didn't come to the Roland on Sunday," Otto says, still pressing me close with his body.

"I couldn't. I had to go see Hans in the hospital."

"You just went to Metz and back for the weekend?" Robert asks. "Do you think we'll believe that?"

"I *did* go," I say, but my voice sounds weak. "Hans is not well. He lost his right arm."

There is a flicker in Otto's eyes and for a moment I hope he'll let go of me. But he adjusts his grip.

"You know what happened yesterday?"

"No."

"We broke into the villa in Tiergarten and collected some stuff. When we came out of the house the police were waiting for us. We managed to run away, but Emil was taken to the police station and now he is waiting to see the judge."

"I'm sorry," I say.

"You certainly should be sorry!" Otto says.

"My little brother is in prison because of you!" Robert says. "And now you will pay for what you did."

"But I had nothing to do with this."

"How else would the police have known that we would come out of the house?"

"It wasn't me who told them. I was worried about Hans."

"Look at this." Otto finally lets go of me and pulls a roll of paper out of his breast pocket. He unrolls it. "Do you recognize this?"

"It looks like the paper that food stamps are printed on," I say.

"That's exactly what it is," Robert says.

"Where did you get this?" I ask.

"Let's say that we have a special friend in the Food Administration," Otto says.

"What are you going to do with it?"

"It's what *you* are going to do with it," Otto says, smiling at me.

"*You* will print some extra food stamps," Robert says. "You are a printer, aren't you?"

I try to step away but Otto pulls me back in front of him. He is so close that I can smell the onion on his breath. "But I can't print anything other than the newspaper. My boss is always with me," I say.

"We watched the printshop and know the timings. The late shift leaves at eleven at night and the early shift doesn't come before three in the morning. That gives you enough time to print the cards we need."

"But if I get caught I'll lose my job," I say.

"Then make sure that you don't get caught," Otto says.

"I can't do it," I say.

"You will! We'll meet at the Roland Fountain next Sunday at three. Bring the ration cards then," Robert says.

Otto presses his large hand against my chest. I step back until I feel the wall behind me. "You should do what we tell you!" he says, wagging his finger in front of my face.

"We know where to find you!" Robert adds before they walk away.

twenty-two

After they have disappeared around the corner I bend down to pick up my keys. My hands are trembling not just from the cold. I walk slowly up to our apartment. Old Moser would find out if anyone uses the print sets without his supervision. I can't print these cards for them. I need to talk the boys out of this. Maybe I could ruin the paper with a big blotch of ink. But then Otto would suspect that I did it on purpose. Before Sunday I have to come up with a better plan.

"There you are! I was starting to worry about you." Hedwig greets me at the door. "Mama is in the kitchen."

"She's here?" I ask. "How come she's not at Aunt Martha's anymore?"

"It seems like they have given up observing me when I leave the house. So Mama thought she could come home."

"Mama," I call, and fall into her arms.

"Moritz, my boy," she says. "You are ice-cold. Come and hold your hands over the fire."

I let her lead me to the stove and begin to rub my hands together over the stove top. "Are you sure you are safe here?" I ask. "Maybe the policeman was just sick."

"Well, there are so many of us now that I think they have given up on individual surveillances." She shrugs.

Mama pulls a chair from the kitchen table and sits down. She motions us to also take a seat and then nods. "Hedwig told me you went to see Hans. That was very brave of you," she says. "How is he?"

I have to swallow before I can speak. "He's blind in one eye and has lost his right arm below the elbow. He couldn't speak and he couldn't see since his eyes were covered. But the nurse said that he will recover." The logs in the oven rearrange themselves with a loud crack and rustle.

"Did they say when he would come home?"

"The nurse said he would have to spend some time in a rehabilitation home after his release from the hospital. She said he had to overcome the shock."

Mama massages her face with her hands. Hedwig has her arms wrapped around herself, as if she is giving herself a hug. There is just the sound of the rain drumming against the windowpane.

After what seems like a long time Mama looks up. Her

face looks strained, older. She whispers, "That's all we get from this damn war. Pain and more pain."

Then Mama takes one deep breath, gets up, and puts on her cardigan.

"Where are you going?" I ask.

"I'm going over to Fox's Pub. Our reading group meets there tonight."

"Reading group?" I ask.

"Just a group of women reading the same book and talking about it," Hedwig says. "I'm going, too."

"You're not going to one of these party meetings again, right?" I ask Mama.

"No, it's just a reading group, boy. Women sitting and talking. That's it!"

"I hope you're done now with these party meetings, anyway," I say.

"At least they won't be illegal much longer," Hedwig says.

"Yes, it is just a question of time," Mama adds.

"What?" I ask.

"The end of the monarchy. The advent of peace and democratic elections," Mama says.

"I can't believe you're still talking like this. The police almost caught you. Was this not enough to scare you? They've been watching our house!"

"Moritz, nothing has changed. Germany is still at war. Lives are lost in senseless battles. The Kaiser and his group of handlers and noblemen are still in charge. We still don't have enough to eat."

"Aren't you feeling bad for Hans?"

"Yes, Moritz. I feel terrible for Hans. I wish I could see him soon. I love your brother. It was not his fault that he became a cripple through the war." She looks at me and I shudder when she says the word "cripple."

"When he comes back we will take care of him as well as we can. He will be proud to see the new Germany," she says.

"But he will only see it with one eye!" I scream.

Mama buttons her cardigan. When she looks up again tears glisten in her eyes. "I know," she says quietly. "I wish it wasn't like this."

"Me too," I whisper, and turn away.

twenty-three

The gaslight sizzles and then blinks, leaving the kitchen in the dark for short moments. Mama and Hedwig have left, but I stand there, staring at the wall. I don't want to stay in the apartment, where Oma will call for me soon. I want to move, run, go somewhere. Fox's Pub is only three blocks away. I pick up my jacket, put on my cap, and walk briskly through the damp evening cold. I know that the pub's meeting room and stage are in the back. Some years ago I came here with Mama, Papa, Hans, Hedwig, and Louise for a Christmas family celebration. I remember the tall Christmas tree and how Louise squeezed my hand when St. Nicholas appeared on stage. When I open the back door a man stops me, pushing his right hand against my chest. "What do you want?"

"I'm Anna Schmidt's son," I say, hoping he won't call her to verify my statement.

He lets me pass and I enter quickly into a corridor that ends with a door labeled STAGE. I open the door and slip between the folds of the thick curtain that hangs behind the stage and frames it on both sides. From here I can see the back of a man standing at a podium, addressing the crowd in the hall. Next to the podium, Mama and two men sit at a long table that is draped with red cloth. This is not a women's reading group. The man asks everyone to take a seat and begins to speak. "The sailors in Kiel and Wilhelmshaven have refused to follow the orders of their commanding officers to embark on a suicide mission against the British navy. Local garrisons and workers have joined this naval mutiny. They have formed councils of workers and sailors and have taken control of the two cities." The audience cheers before he continues: "The Kaiser has to abdicate or the revolution will sweep him away!"

Next, he introduces Mama, calling her "Comrade Schmidt." The people in the audience greet her with applause as she moves to the podium. "The time of despotism and war profiteers is over. Too many workers have perished on the battlefield while profiteers stuff their pockets. Too many children have starved while men in suits grow bellies . . ." The room erupts in cheers and applause. I think of Hans and what the war did to him. I think of the filled pantry in the villa and the little girl's face staring at the fat director's sandwich in the Food Administration's office. I slowly clap my hands together, but the applause has already ebbed and Mama continues:

"Sailors and workers are on their way to Berlin. It can only be a matter of time until they reach the capital. We should be prepared to greet them with open arms. We need to organize a mass strike and distribute enough weapons to take the palace and major centers of power."

Suddenly, there is a commotion in the hall. I don't dare to leave my spot behind the curtain for fear of being discovered, but I hear a voice call, "Police!" I move the curtain aside just an inch to see that the people who had sat in the audience are rushing toward the doors. But the room quickly fills with policemen. Several participants are being handcuffed. I can find neither Mama nor Hedwig and hope they have escaped already. Keeping close to the curtain, I carefully move to the side of the stage, taking an occasional peek through to see where the policemen are. There is Mama! A policeman is holding her by the arm while a second one is putting handcuffs on her. I want to step out from behind the curtains and yell her name. But the policemen have already turned her around and are shoving her toward the entrance. Hedwig calls after Mama, until a policeman also grabs hold of her. I watch as they both disappear through the front door.

I need to find a better place to hide. The police will soon be up on the stage and when they go through the curtain layers they will find me. I scan the floor and notice a trapdoor. I try the handle and it opens easily. There is a short ladder leading to a dark space under the stage. As I climb down the ladder, the curtain rustles. I look up to see women's boots and the hem of a skirt next to me. I can't see a face as the person crouches down, trying to hide in a fold of the curtain.

"Hello?" I whisper. She turns around and I recognize the girl I met on the train. "Rebecca?"

She turns her head. "Who is this?"

"It's me, Moritz!" I whisper, and take one step up on the ladder so she can see me.

"Moritz? What are you doing here?"

"Come quick! We can hide under the stage," I say, and hold out my hand to help her onto the ladder. She quickly climbs down and I pull the trapdoor shut. Seconds later we hear the thumping of police boots passing over our heads, followed by a voice calling, "Heinrich! I thought I saw someone up here onstage behind the curtains."

"They must have gotten away," another policeman answers.

"Let's go then. The ones we have caught need to be taken to the station."

"All right. I'm coming." We can hear the policeman walk away. Then it is quiet.

twenty-four

Thank you!" Rebecca whispers. "What are you doing here?"

"They caught my mother and my sister," I say.

"Oh, no!" she says. "I'm sorry. What are their names?"

"Anna and Hedwig Schmidt," I say, imagining Mama and Hedwig in a big police van, handcuffed, being herded to the police station.

"You are Anna Schmidt's son?" Rebecca asks, and there is admiration in her voice.

I nod but then remember that she can't see me. "Yes, Anna Schmidt is my mother. She was hiding in my aunt's apartment until today and now the police caught her because she had to attend this meeting."

"We can talk to my boss, Hugo Haase," Rebecca says.

"Hugo Haase, the member of parliament?" I ask. "He's your boss?"

"I work in his legal office," she says. "You should come to speak to him tomorrow."

"You think he could do something for them?"

"He's a lawyer and often defends social democrats in court."

"What were you doing here?" I ask. "Did you just come to hear the speeches?"

"I was going to bring some flyers. But my train got in late and then I had to wait at the printshop," she says.

"It was your luck that you came late," I say.

"My luck was that you saved me!" she says.

"No problem," I mumble.

"How is your brother?" she asks.

"Not well," I say.

"I'm sorry," she says. "You said he was badly injured."

"It was terrible to see him. His eye and one arm half gone. He used to be a good watchmaker." I stop. In the darkness she won't see the tears welling in my eyes, but I am sure she can hear the strain in my voice. I swallow.

"That must have been horrible," she says. "Will he come home soon?"

"It'll be a while, most likely," I say.

"At least he won't have to go back to the front," she says.

"The war is almost over," I say. "And we lost."

"This war shouldn't have started in the first place. Nothing is ever gained from war," she says. I wipe my eyes with my sleeve and nod in the darkness. Then a short silence falls between us.

"I think we can go back up. It's all quiet up there." I

pull myself up and slide my hand along the wall to find the ladder.

"Where are you?" I feel her hand on my shin. "Ah! There you are," she says. "Let's get out of here!"

"Wait!" Her touch has sent an electric current through my body that is now heating up my face. I try to breathe calmly to let the color drain from my face before we step into the light. I climb the ladder, find the handle, and push the trapdoor open. A shaft of light sails down from the stage and I step up, turn around, and hold out my hand to her.

"I'm glad the police didn't get my flyers. They would really have liked to confiscate those. Thank you for helping the cause," she says, pointing to a small basket she carries over her arm.

"I was helping *you*," I say.

We step through the curtain and look out across the empty room. I wonder where Mama and Hedwig are now.

"You won't be able to do anything for them tonight," Rebecca says. "You should come to Hugo Haase's office tomorrow. I'll tell him about you. What time do you get off work?"

"At four," I say.

"Then I'll see you at a quarter past four at Zimmerstrasse 80," she says.

twenty-five

Back at our apartment I try to walk quietly past Oma's room, but a squeaking floorboard in the hallway gives me away.

"Moooooritz!" Oma calls.

"How are you, Oma?" I enter her room. The rancid smell takes my breath for a moment.

"My rheumatism is very bad today," she whines from her bed. "It's the rain."

"Let's open the window just a bit," I say. "Doctors say now that fresh air is the best cure for rheumatism."

"No, no, no," she complains. "My own grandson tortures me." With a sigh Oma turns her head toward the wall.

"I'm not torturing you, Oma!" I move a chair closer to her bed. On a plate lies a piece of dry bread, untouched, the edges bent slightly upward. "Have you eaten anything today?"

"I can't!" she moans.

"How about some tea?"

"No!" She turns around and grabs my arm with her bony hand. "Can you get the camphor?"

"I don't think we have any camphor," I lie. Usually, Mama rubs Oma's back with camphor when she complains about pain.

"I think I saw the bottle in the bathroom, just today." Oma's watery eyes focus on me. "Please get it and rub my back."

There is no way out. I fetch the bottle from the bathroom together with a towel. When I return, Oma, still lying in bed, tries to pull her dress and undershirt up.

"That won't work, Oma!" I say. "You need to sit up."

"Help me, then!"

I bend over and prop her against the pillow.

"Now lift the dress and undershirt. Bend forward!"

I sprinkle some of the liquid onto her wrinkled skin.

"My hands are cold," I warn her. "Don't be surprised!"

With my right hand I begin to rub the camphor over Oma's upper back. Her wrinkled skin feels like parchment under my touch. I wish Mama or Hedwig were here to do this.

"Don't touch me!" she suddenly screams, jerking away from me.

"How am I supposed to rub your back if I don't touch you?" I ask.

But Oma has pulled her knees up to her chin and wraps the blanket tightly around her.

"No, I don't want you to touch me! Leave me alone!"

"Well." I step back from her bed and lift my arms. "I'm not touching you!"

"Go away!"

"I'm going away!" I say, closing the door behind me.

I throw myself onto my bed. Why did Mama and Hedwig have to do this? Now I am alone with Oma. How am I supposed to take care of her all by myself! I need all my energy to solve the problem Otto has brought on with his threat and deadline. I hope Hugo Haase can help me quickly.

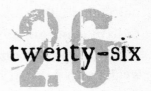

twenty-six

A brass sign directs visitors to Hugo Haase's legal office on the second floor. I ring the bell twice before I can hear footsteps on the wooden parquet.

"Come in," Rebecca says as she opens the door. I follow her through a long corridor, watching a thin lock of hair on the nape of her neck bouncing off her white collar. She leads me into an office with two windows looking out onto the street.

"Did you read the book?" she asks.

"Yes, I did."

"And do you feel like a traitor now?" She looks at me with a smirk that makes those cute dimples appear on her cheeks again.

"No, I don't feel like a traitor," I say, hoping my smile looks amused and not forced. "The book was good. Not as good as the previous Winnetous but good enough."

"I'll let him know that you're here," she says, and motions for me to take a seat in the chair next to the door.

I sit down and look around the room. The walls are painted a light shade of yellow. A tile oven behind me radiates warmth, and I recognize the thermos Rebecca had on the train standing on the desk next to a typewriter.

"He's ready to see you," she says.

"*Guten Tag,* Moritz!" Hugo Haase gets up from a leather chair and shakes my hand firmly. He is only a bit taller than me and from close up he seems older than he did during his speech.

"Take a seat. We only have enough fuel to heat one room. So we're keeping Rebecca's office warm since she spends more time here than I do."

When I sit down on the chair across from him I can feel the cool leather through my pants. Behind his desk stands a shelf filled with leather-bound volumes. Next to the door hangs a framed print of an old map. I recognize the outline of Eastern Prussia. Through the window I see the rain bombarding the last remaining yellow leaves of a chestnut tree.

"Rebecca has told me why you're here. I'm sorry that they caught your mother and your sister. But let me tell you, they are in good spirits."

"How do you know?"

"I went to the police station this morning," Hugo Haase says. "We are expecting amnesty for all political prisoners soon and in the current political climate the

authorities might not want to incarcerate more comrades."

"What does that mean?"

"That means they will not be held for very long. Don't worry!"

"Can I see them?"

"No," he says, massaging the bridge of his nose. "I'm afraid not. You have to be an officer of the court to be allowed to speak to prisoners. But we will send one of my associates, and Rebecca can keep you informed."

"Thank you very much," I say. "Please let them know that I am taking care of my grandmother."

"They will appreciate that," he says, and gets up.

At the door to the front office he shakes my hand. "Goodbye, Moritz! Don't worry about your mother and sister. We'll get them out soon," he says.

"Thank you," I say.

Rebecca is wearing her coat and puts the thermos in her bag.

"Goodbye, Dr. Haase," she says. "And good luck in Kiel!"

"Thank you, Rebecca! You have a nice evening now," he says, and disappears into his room again.

"Is he traveling?" I ask.

"Yes," she says. "He wants to go to Kiel to talk to the sailors. You heard about the mutiny?"

"I've read about it, and in her speech yesterday my mother said that the sailors are on their way to Berlin," I say. "Do you think that's true?"

"Oh, yes!" she says, and looks at me, surprised. "The revolution has started. It's rolling across the country!" Her eyes glisten with enthusiasm just like Mama's and Hedwig's when they talk about the upcoming revolt.

"Where do you live?" I say.

"We can walk together," she says. "I live just a block down. It's on the way to the subway."

As we walk down the sidewalk, passing a queue of women and children lined up in front of a dairy store, I wonder if I could ask her for another book. But that would probably be too forward.

"Would you like to get another book?" Rebecca asks, as if reading my mind. "My father owns a bookstore with a small library attached. I could recommend something."

"Yes," I say. "That would be nice."

She stops in front of a redbrick building. A door opens onto a narrow room with high ceilings, its walls covered with bookshelves. Behind a desk at the back of the store sits an older man with a small black yarmulke on top of his curly white hair. He gets up to greet us.

"Good evening," he says.

"Father, this is Moritz Schmidt, the son of Anna Schmidt, who was captured by the police last night." Rebecca turns to me. "Moritz, this is Nathan Cohen, my father."

"Oh." Her father lifts his eyebrows and shakes my hand firmly. "Very pleased to meet you."

"Nice to meet you, too," I say.

"Rebecca has told me what you did for her last night.

Thank you very much for saving her. I tell her to be more careful, but she doesn't want to listen," he says.

"Moritz likes to read. I gave him my latest Winnetou, but he prefers authors that haven't traveled to an enemy country," she says, smiling at me.

"Maybe he would like one of these," Herr Cohen says, and points to a stack of books on a small table next to his desk.

"Oh, yes," Rebecca says. "Those are new. We just cataloged them for our small library. You should fill out a card to become a member."

The bell above the entrance rings and we all turn to see a man enter the store. He wears a thick felt jacket and a red wool scarf. "You are early," Herr Cohen says, and glances at the clock on the wall. "I have to do it now," the man says, looking at me suspiciously. Herr Cohen ushers him to the back room from where I can only hear them whisper.

"Rebecca, would you come here for a minute?" Herr Cohen asks.

"I'll leave you alone with these books. I'll be right back," she says, before she also disappears into the back room.

I browse the bookshelves while I wait for her to return.

"We are getting a delivery right now," Rebecca says when she comes back. "My father has to close the store for a moment while we are carrying the boxes through the back door."

"No problem," I say. "Do you need any help?"

She hesitates for a moment. "Yes, we would appreciate it. It will be faster with more help. If you don't mind."

I follow her to the backyard, where the man in the red scarf is backing up a small truck against the rear entrance. HENKE'S TOWEL SERVICE is printed on the side door.

"How many do you have, Anton?" Herr Cohen asks.

"Just five, this time," says the man in the red scarf, and climbs onto the back of the truck from where he hands me the first crate. "Careful, son," he says. "They are heavy."

"What's inside these?" I ask.

"Books," Rebecca says quickly.

"Where should I put them?" I ask Herr Cohen.

"Please bring them downstairs." He opens the door to the basement. I carefully balance my load down the steps and place it near the wall. In the dim light I can make out another pile of similar boxes in the corner. When the five crates are stored downstairs Anton tips the edge of his cap and climbs back into the cab of his truck.

"Bye, Anton," Herr Cohen calls, and waves while Anton quickly drives away.

"Thank you very much!" Rebecca says. "Now let's get you a book. How about this one? *Gustaf Adolf's Page.* It's about a girl disguised as a boy who defends her king." She holds up the book.

"I'll take it," I say.

"I hope you'll come back soon." She looks directly at me, smiling.

I nod, pressing the book a little harder in front of my chest before I say, "I will." Then I turn around before the tingling feeling in my stomach makes me blush again.

twenty-seven

Frau Haller, who lives in the apartment below ours, has told me that the butcher is selling sausages. After I feed Oma a light supper that she eats without much fuss, I put on another sweater to protect myself from the cold, damp weather while I stand in line. The paper Otto has given me is lying in my drawer. Even if I take the risk of using the typesetting machine for something other than the newspaper, the cards wouldn't come out right. Most likely store owners would notice the fraud right away and notify the police. Maybe I should just print them and then let Otto and Robert get caught by the police for using fraudulent ration cards. But if Old Moser finds out, and he will, I'll lose my job. I still have four days to solve the problem. Before I leave I slip the book into my pocket to read while I am waiting in the queue. The faster I finish the book the sooner I can return to Rebecca's library for a new one.

When I turn the corner, Otto is waiting for me, smiling broadly as if I were his long-lost friend. "How are you?" he asks, and pats my shoulder with his square hand.

"I have to go to the butcher. They have sausage and I have ration cards," I say.

"Are those the ration cards that you printed yourself?"

"No," I say. "I've been meaning to talk to you about this. I can't do it!"

"What do you mean you can't do it?" Otto says.

"I cannot falsify those cards," I say. "I don't want to do it!"

"That's exactly what I was worried about," he says, and rubs his hands together as if he is about to make an important announcement. "That's why I was on my way to talk to you. In fact, I wanted to talk to you yesterday, but you were busy with your new girlfriend."

"I don't have a girlfriend," I say.

"I think her name is Rebecca Cohen," he says.

"How do you know her?"

"We followed you and noticed that you went to her father's store."

"He runs a library and I got a book. It's right here," I say.

"But you also helped them carry crates with weapons into their basement," Otto says. His face looks angry now.

"Weapons? Those were book boxes!" I say. Suddenly there is a hollow feeling in my stomach.

"That's maybe what they told you," Otto says, "but why would books be delivered by a towel service?" He shakes his head and looks at me with a mock frown. "No, no, no, my friend. These people are planning an uprising against the government and you helped them. Robert knows someone that works at this towel service who ratted on Anton. And now I am here, helping you to make the right decision. I expect the police would be very interested to find out what your friend's family has in their basement."

"But I can't do it. If I get caught—" I say, but Otto interrupts me.

"I'm sure you wouldn't want to see your friends in jail?" He steps back. "I'll give you one more day. We're planning another operation tomorrow night."

"What are you going to do tomorrow night?" I ask.

"Robert found a way to get into that fancy grocery store at Tiergartenstrasse, where all the rich people buy. They probably have an interesting basement!" Otto says, and I nod. "I'll expect you at the Roland at nine, with the ration cards! If you're not there, we will go to the police and tell them about the little bookstore where your girlfriend works!"

"All right," I say. "I'll be there, with the cards." Even though I know that I won't.

twenty-eight

I need to see Rebecca. I run down to the subway and jump into the last compartment just before the doors close. In my mind I replay Otto's threat, and it's hard to concentrate on reading my book. I get off at Kochstrasse station, take the stairs two at a time, and run the last block down her street. I am relieved to see light in her father's bookstore. When I enter, Rebecca is standing in front of a ladder, sorting books from a box.

"Hello," she says. "You look upset."

"Why did you lie to me?"

"About what?"

"About the boxes. There were weapons inside those crates and you told me they were filled with books!"

She averts her eyes. "I'm sorry," she says. "I should

have told you the truth. But I wasn't sure if we could trust you."

"Why do you need weapons, anyway? I thought you were against war and violence."

"We are against the war, but we are fighting against a reigning military dictatorship that is ruining this country," she says. "And they won't give in easily." I remember how quick she was with words when we talked about Karl May on the train and decide not to argue any further.

"Well, you should have told me that I was helping you to hide *weapons* in your store!" I say, my voice louder than I intend it to be.

"My father thought you were one of us because you are Anna's son," she says.

I want to say that I am not one of *them*, but suddenly I am not so sure anymore.

"How did you find out?" she asks.

"A friend of my brother's just came to see me. He followed us yesterday and he knew that Anton delivered weapons out of the ammunition factory hidden in the towel truck. He will tell the police," I say.

"Oh, no!" She throws her hands in front of her face. "They know that Anton delivers weapons?"

I nod. "And they have already turned him in to the police. You and your father should shift the crates to another place."

"But my father is not here right now. He is at the

synagogue and won't be back for another hour or so," she says.

"Is there someone else with a car or carriage who could come and take them?" I ask.

"I have to make a phone call. I know someone from the party committee who could help us," she says.

"Good," I say, and then I hear myself add, "I'll help."

I carry the boxes back upstairs and place them by the back door. Rebecca returns from the phone. "Wilhelm, Hugo Haase's driver, will come with a car and transport the crates to another location," she says. I stack the last box on the pile and close the door to the basement.

Soon after, a black automobile stops in the backyard. The driver is a massive older man with a shock of white hair. I open the back door and Rebecca introduces us. "This is Moritz Schmidt. He came to tell me that someone has ratted on Anton. Moritz, this is Wilhelm." He offers me his huge hand and I see mine disappear in his firm grip.

"Any relation to Anna Schmidt?" Wilhelm asks.

"She's my mother," I say.

He nods approvingly and then grabs a box. "I knew this would happen," he says. "The closer you come to the revolution the fewer people you can trust."

"Thank you for coming so quickly," Rebecca says.

"No problem," Wilhelm says. "I'll store them in our bedroom for now. Won't be very long, and should the police come, my wife, Bertha, won't let them past the threshold." He breaks out with a deep laugh.

We finish carrying the boxes to the backseat of the

motorcar. Wilhelm shakes Rebecca's hand and waves to me before he leaves.

"Thank you so much," Rebecca says after the car has disappeared. She throws her arms around my neck. I don't move, letting the touch of her ear on my cheek radiate through my body.

twenty-nine

You had quite an exciting few days, I understand," Herr Goldmann says when I stop by his office. "I heard that your mother and sister have been taken by the police?"

"Yes," I say. "The police call it 'protective custody,' but I received a message from Hugo Haase that they would be released tomorrow."

"Good," Herr Goldmann says. "But how do you know Hugo Haase?"

"As a lawyer he helps social democrats who have trouble with the law. And I also know his secretary," I say.

"I don't know if I'd have the courage to do what your mother does," Herr Goldmann says.

"What?"

"Risk my own freedom to fight for the freedom of others," Herr Goldmann says. "Don't you think this is remarkable?" Herr Goldmann pulls up his eyebrows and blows out a cloud of smoke.

"She was different before the war," I say. "We used to be just a normal family."

"Imagine what she has been through," Herr Goldmann says. "First she lost her husband. Then her young daughter died. And now her oldest son is maimed." He shakes his head. "And like so many other women she has to work in a factory to earn enough to feed you and your sister and your grandmother. Where does she get the strength to go out and fight? If this had happened to me I would want to crawl into a hole. Your mother is a remarkable lady!"

"I guess you're right," I say quietly. Suddenly I feel embarrassed that Herr Goldmann has had to explain to me how extraordinary Mama is.

Herr Kirchner, the editor in chief, stops at Herr Goldmann's desk. "Now that the Kaiser has left Berlin and the revolution is on its way, I wonder if we soon will live in a Bolshevik state."

"I don't think so," Herr Goldmann says. "The majority of social democrats are with Ebert, who wants a democracy with elections for a National Assembly as soon as possible. They don't want the Soviet model. But first of all we need to end this war."

Herr Kirchner nods. "I hope you're right. If we comply with Wilson's conditions for peace, the armistice should be reached soon."

Herr Goldmann turns to me. "This is Moritz. He works

in the printshop, but I see a lot of promise in him as a writer."

Herr Kirchner shakes my hand and laughs. "Look, Aaron, you made him blush! Don't be shy, young man." Herr Kirchner pats my shoulder. "If Aaron thinks you can write I would believe him."

After Herr Kirchner has left, Herr Goldmann gets up. "I have to go to my next assignment. Keep your eyes open for more stories. They are everywhere!"

"I have a question," I say, lowering my voice.

"Go ahead, my friend," Herr Goldmann says.

"How would I leave an anonymous tip with the police if I knew about a break-in that is about to happen?"

"Hmmm." Herr Goldmann lifts his eyebrows. "I assume you wouldn't tell me how you happen to know."

"No," I say. "It has to be an anonymous tip. I thought the police reporter might have some connections."

"He sure does," Herr Goldmann says. "Let me introduce you to him and you can deliver your information to him in person."

thirty

I place the two packs of cigarettes the police reporter gave me on the kitchen table. The article was in today's paper. Two young men were jailed after they were caught in the act as they tried to break into Behnke's Grocery at Tiergartenstrasse. At home I read the article one more time before I stuff the newspaper under the kindling to light the fire. While I watch the flame sizzle through the paper, I remember the day I stole Adolf Renner's sandwich. During math time in fifth grade my stomach grumbled but I had forgotten my sandwich. I knew Alfred always had good sausage sandwiches since his mother helped out at the butcher's. The recess bell rang and he dashed to the bathroom down the hall. As the other pupils left the classroom, I bent down, opened his schoolbag, took out the small package, unwrapped the brown paper, and wolfed down the sandwich in a few bites. Then I ran to the upstairs bathroom before he returned. After I had washed out my mouth I sauntered down to the schoolyard, where I found Adolf crying. I couldn't go over to talk to him; instead I spent the rest of recess in the classroom and faked a stomachache when Adolf returned so I didn't have to sit next to him. Now, as I put the lid on the stove and hang the stoker next to the oven, the same throbbing of guilt rushes through me. But I push the feeling aside. It was the right thing to do. I couldn't let them hurt Rebecca. I couldn't risk losing my job by printing those cards.

~⁂~

The fire is crackling in the stove when I hear Mama and Hedwig at the door.

"It's good to be home," Mama says. "You even found wood. It's nice and warm in here." She rubs her hands together and takes off her coat.

"Anna?" Oma calls from her room.

"Yes, Mother!" Mama opens the door to the unlit room where Oma sits in her chair, next to the tile oven, wrapped in a blanket.

"Anna. There you are! Did you bring some meat? After you stood in line for such a long time I hope you got a good piece of rump."

"You didn't tell her where I was?" Mama looks at me.

"I did. But it didn't register," I say.

Mama bends down to give Oma a hug. "You smell sour, Anna! And Hedwig. I haven't seen you all day!"

"We'll see you at dinner," Mama says as we leave Oma's room.

"She's right," Hedwig says. "We do smell sour."

"Everybody does these days," Mama says. "There is no soap on sale anywhere."

"What's this?" Hedwig asks, holding up the two packs of cigarettes.

"Those are mine," I say.

"You don't smoke," Mama says.

"I got them at work," I say.

"We could trade these for soap," Hedwig says. "What do you think, little brother? Wouldn't you like the women in the house to smell better?"

"I don't know," I say, wishing I had kept the cigarettes in my pocket.

"Moritz," Mama says, "soap would be good to have. Even for yourself."

"Maybe." I look at the cigarettes, thinking about their suggestion, when we hear footsteps in the hallway.

"Hans," Mama calls, and gasps. My brother stands in the doorway. He wears a black patch over his left eye. The skin on his cheeks has healed some but his good looks are destroyed. The sleeve of his jacket is folded back above the right elbow.

"Hello," he says, and Mama opens her arms to an embrace. Before she lets him go Mama holds him at arm's length, studying his face. With her left finger she touches the scar on his cheek. "Oh, my boy!" she whispers, and a tear glides down her cheek.

Hedwig still holds her hand over her mouth. "This is the way I'll look from now on," Hans says, stepping closer to her. "You might as well get used to it." When they hug she sobs into his shoulder.

Next he turns to me. "Thank you for visiting me," he says. The scar on his upper lip distorts his smile. When we embrace, the stump of his arm touches my sleeve and I shudder.

"I didn't expect you back so soon. Did they officially release you from the hospital already?" Mama asks.

"No," Hans says. "I was supposed to stay longer. But when I heard that all patients were going to be moved to another clinic away from the front I made my way to the train station in Metz." He shakes his head. "I didn't want to be in a hospital anymore. Enough of nurses and doctors and other wounded bastards like myself."

Mama dabs her face with a handkerchief. Her eyes are red and swollen.

"You are so thin, my boy," she says. "I wish I had something special to cook for you, but dinner will be soggy war bread with the ends of blood sausage that I got for this week's meat ration cards."

"That's all right," Hans says. "It's not that they spoiled me in the army. But I am as hungry as a bear.

"Wow," he says, and reaches for the cigarettes. "Real tobacco cigarettes." He opens one of the packs, shakes out a cigarette, and lights it with his left hand. "I didn't know you had picked up smoking."

❧

Hedwig and Mama quickly set the supper table, and when we sit down Hans ravishes the food like a famished animal. I can tell that Mama and Hedwig take less to make sure there is enough for him. Mama asks about the food he ate during the war and Hans thanks her for the packages, describes stews and cold canned food. Yet the conversation feels strained. Hedwig just stares at her plate, and when she does look at Hans she nods as if she is hard of hearing and they are talking over a great distance. Mama keeps moving her hand behind her ear to fasten a strand of hair that has loosened. Then there is only the sound of Hans smacking his lips and swallowing the sausage. It is not that warm in the kitchen, but with an awkward movement Hans takes off his shirt and continues to eat in his undershirt. I try not to look at his stump, but it hangs right next to my left elbow. The end of the upper arm is round and red with a thick pinkish scar slithering across.

I see Hedwig peeking at it, shooting short glances to the other end of the table.

"Stop staring at me!" Hans yells.

"Hans," Mama says in her softest voice. "No one is staring at you."

She reaches for his left hand, but he pulls away.

Suddenly, with a rustling sound, Oma appears in her doorway. She points her bony finger at Hans and asks, "Who is this?"

Hans gets up and leaves for our bedroom.

thirty-one

I follow Hans a few minutes later. When I open the door
he kicks a box under his bed with the heel of his shoe.
Then he quickly tries to hide something under his pillow.
His shirt is rolled up a bit and I can see a small trickle of
blood on his stomach. "You're bleeding," I say.

"That's nothing," he says, and presses his shirt down
on the spot.

"What's in the box under the bed?"

"My medication."

Then he pulls a syringe from under the pillowcase.
"Since we are staying in the same room, you'll see it sooner
or later anyway," he says.

"What is this?" I ask.

"It's morphine," he says. "It helps me with the pain."
He bends down and opens the box. Inside are two rows
of small brown glass vials.

"How long will you have to take it?"

"I don't know." He shrugs.

I sit down on my bed and for a moment we are just looking at different spots on the floor. I worry about the return of the awkward silence, but then I have an idea.

"We could go and see a movie. There is a new Pola Negri film playing at the cinema," I say. "I have money for two tickets. You might like to get out of here for a while."

"All right," Hans says, and stuffs his shirt into his pants. He gets up and lifts his jacket with his left arm, trying to glide his stump into the sleeve. I step forward to hold the other end of the jacket for him, but he pulls away. "Leave me alone," he yells. "I can do this myself."

Before the main film starts, the weekly newsreel shows us scenes from the war. According to the text that flickers in white letters on a black background the enemy has difficulties defending itself against the strength of the German army. Black-and-white images show tanks advancing toward enemy lines. In the background grenades fall and explode with white plumes of smoke. The next sequence shows the Kaiser and the empress on a visit to a field hospital. The empress gives a wounded soldier a bouquet of flowers with a gloved hand while the Kaiser, clad in his military uniform, nods solemnly.

Suddenly, Hans gets up and walks toward the exit. I assume he has to use the washroom and I focus on an advertisement for tonic that, if gargled, promises to protect the user from the Spanish flu.

The lights go on and a girl with a tray strapped around her waist offers ersatz chocolate. I wave to her and buy two bars. When the lights dim again and the movie is about to begin, Hans still has not returned to his seat. I get up to look for him in the washroom. Inside I hear sobbing from one of the stalls. "Hans," I call. "Hans. Are you in there?" I knock. The door opens and Hans steps out, his face swollen and wet.

"Hans, are you all right?"

He bends over the washbasin, cups cold water with his left hand, and lets it run over his face.

"Are you in pain?" I ask, feeling small and helpless.

He just groans. "I am never without pain. I haven't been without pain for two months, since this happened to me."

"I'm sorry," I say. Hans now leans with his back against the washbasin, his eye focused on the frosted glass of the washroom window.

"Look, I bought chocolate, or ersatz chocolate, rather," I say, holding out the palm of my hand with the two small rectangles wrapped in yellow paper.

"I don't want any chocolate," he says, and brushes my hand aside.

"Would you like to go back in and watch the movie?"

"No," he says. "I want to go home and go to bed."

While we walk through the rain we don't talk, and I wish I hadn't asked him to go to the movies.

At home we hear Hedwig's and Mama's voices in the

living room as we hang up our jackets at the door. When we enter, Hedwig asks, "Was it sold out?"

"No, I changed my mind. I'm too tired to watch a movie," Hans says before he disappears into the bedroom without wishing us good night. I stay with Mama and Hedwig in the living room. "He's in pain," I say, and Mama nods. "It will take a while until he feels like a part of us again," she says.

"He should probably see a doctor if he has left the hospital without permission," Hedwig says. I think about the morphine, but I don't want to mention it. Mama continues to read, Hedwig picks up her darning, and I put my journal on my lap. I try to write but nothing will come onto the paper. How many times have I imagined Hans's return? Now that he's here, it's all so different from what I thought it would be. When I get up I feel something in my pocket. I pull the two melted ersatz chocolate bars out and throw them in the fire on my way to the bedroom.

thirty-two

I'm awakened by Hans's screams. "No! No! No!"

I get up and shake his shoulder until his eye opens. "Wake up, Hans! You're having a nightmare," I say. "It's all right."

He groans and sits up. "Nothing is all right," he says.

I climb back under my own covers and listen in the darkness. Then I ask: "Do you want to talk about what it was like? In the war, I mean."

"No," he says quickly. "You wouldn't understand. It was horrible." He breathes heavily and already I wish I hadn't asked. But then he continues. "Always waiting, trying not to think of what could happen. After an attack you hear the screams of the wounded. The wailing of the dying. The musky smell of blood is everywhere. And the fear. Always the fear."

I can hear him swallow.

"I had this buddy, Hans Kollmann. His name was also Hans. He was from Bamberg, down in Bavaria, rolled his r's when he spoke and said *'Servus'* instead of *'Guten Tag.'* We stayed in the trenches near Amiens together for almost two weeks. The Brits and French bombarded us and then the Americans came to help them. One day we were smoking a cigarette. It was foggy, soup so thick you could hardly see your hand. He told me about a girl he liked back home. Then suddenly, this loud whistling sound came closer and closer, before it hit our trench. I jumped to the left and he jumped to the right. It hit about nine feet to our right. He leaped into it. I called his name but got no answer. At first I didn't see him in the thick fog and smoke. I crept slowly in the direction he had jumped. Then I felt his boot, tugged it. When it was close enough I saw that the lower part of his leg was still in it, only the lower part. A little farther over I touched his hand. It was only his hand. The blast had ripped his body apart. I lay there, soaked in his blood and mine until they came with the stretcher. That was just a week before it hit me."

"I'm sorry," I whisper. Those empty words are the only ones I can think of.

"I told you that you wouldn't understand," he says. "You were here all this time in your nice home. You have no idea." I can hear him fumble for the suitcase under his bed. Then, the scratch of a match, and in the thin light of the candle he takes out one of the brown vials and prepares a syringe. With a sigh he stretches himself out on the bed. Soon after, he snores calmly.

The images of his story lurch through my head. I am still awake when Hans starts to toss in his bed again. There is a low moaning. I get up and take my bedding into the living room to sleep on the sofa.

thirty-three

Hans sits at the kitchen table, balancing a spoonful of oatmeal with his left hand. He has been back now for five days. The spoon trembles in his hand and the oatmeal spills into the bowl. I get up and pour myself a glass of water so that he doesn't feel like I am watching him. But his next attempt fails also and he throws the spoon onto the table.

"Ahhhhhh!" he sighs, and tries to steady his left hand by stretching his fingers. "The tremor is so bad today, I can't get the food in my mouth."

"Let me help you," I say, and I pull my chair closer and feed my brother his oatmeal, spoon after spoon.

"How did the sewing machine get here?" he asks.

"I bought it back for Mama, hoping she would return to sewing," I say.

"But she didn't," Hans says.

"No, she sure didn't," I say, and hope he won't scold me for my naïve faith that the machine would change things.

"Nothing is going to be the way it used to be," he says. I just nod and pass another spoonful of oatmeal to his lips.

"The two of them are really involved in this political stuff," Hans says after he swallows.

"Yes," I say. "They even spent four nights at the police station last week for speaking at an illegal gathering."

"Serves them right," Hans says. "It's all a Bolshevik conspiracy."

"I don't know about that, but it's dangerous, yet they won't let go of it."

"These communists all come from Russia and plan to stage the same Bolshevik revolution they had over there," Hans says, and I can see small beads of sweat collecting on his upper lip.

"Mama and Hedwig are social democrats. They're not communists," I say, but he doesn't seem to hear. "They are fighting for a democratic Germany."

"Communists and Jews—those are the downfall of Germany," Hans says.

I think of Rebecca and say, "Not all Jews are bad people."

"In the bed next to me in the hospital was this old major. Valentin von Ewald. He'd lost his right leg. But he still had both of his eyes and he loved to read. He explained it to me. These socialists, their leaders are all Jews. Rosa Luxemburg. Karl Liebknecht," Hans hisses.

"Maybe," I mumble, wondering if I should point out the differences between communists and social democrats. But I just want to get away from this subject.

"Are you going to look for work?" I ask.

"I sure need to find work," Hans says. "I can't sit around here all day."

"Herr Stahnke, who drives the horses for the coal man, has only one arm. Maybe he can help you to find work," I say.

"You mean one cripple helps another one?" Hans asks in a sharp voice.

"No, that's not what I mean," I say.

"I saw a notice that they are looking for workers at the stockyards," he says. "Shouldn't be too hard to kill animals now, after I've killed people for over a year." He lets out a shrill laugh. The clock above the sink shows a quarter to six. I usually don't walk to the subway before six-thirty, but I push my chair back and tell him that it's time for me to leave for work.

When I return from work in the evening I close the main door behind me and enter the stairway. While my eyes slowly adjust to the darkness I make out the silhouette of a woman sitting on the stairs in front of the mailboxes.

"Frau Haller? What's the matter? Are you all right?" I ask, and gently touch our neighbor's shoulder.

"My boy, Walter, he is dead!" she says, and her body shakes with sobs. "I got the letter. They wrote that he fell for his fatherland and that he was brave until the end. But he was only twenty-one years old. What for?"

"I'm so sorry," I say.

"And for what?" she asks again. "The war is almost over. It can only be a few more days. I was looking forward to seeing him soon, had already traded for some white flour to bake his favorite cake."

Outside on the sidewalk a dog barks, followed by a woman's high-pitched call for him to stop. I shift my weight, searching for words.

"Help me up, will you," she says finally, and I take her arm to gently pull her up. She steadies herself and holds on to the banister.

"Thank you, Moritz."

"Is there anything I can do for you?" I ask.

"No," she says. "Thank you! But be thankful your brother came home."

I nod as we slowly walk upstairs in the dark.

"You're lucky," she says, and sighs.

"I am," I mumble. "Goodbye, Frau Haller."

Hans sits in the living room, next to the tile oven, staring out of the window. "I didn't get the job," he says. "They don't need any cripples to kill cattle either."

"Don't give up yet," I say. "I'm sure you'll find something soon."

"How's your work in the printshop?" he asks.

"Good," I say, and sit down on the seat opposite from him. "They let me write for the paper once in a while."

"You're becoming one of those scribblers?"

"Yes, let me show you." I rush to our bedroom and pull out the cigar box with the articles I have written.

He picks one out and holds it between the thumb and index finger of his left hand. "Hmmm," he says. "Who would have thought my little brother writes! They don't have any real journalists?"

"Herr Goldmann, the editor, likes my writing. He asks me to write small pieces for them," I say. "He thinks I have talent. Remember I wrote to you about it in one of my letters."

"What is this?"

"Oh, that's a poem I wrote for the ninth war bond. There was a contest in the paper but I didn't win."

Hans reads it in a high-pitched voice and draws the words into long syllables:

Our children are starving.
Our women sleep alone.
The allies' grenades are exploding,
scattering our brave men's bones,
but in spite of the enemies' wrath . . .

"It's not very good. I know." I pull the paper away from him.

"My little brother is writing some schmaltzy poem,

while I crouch in a trench as the French and British pound me and my comrades with gas and mortar attacks?"

"I'm sorry," I say. "I just wanted you to see the articles. This poem wasn't very good. I tried to win the prize money so I could buy back the sewing machine for Mama. That's all."

Suddenly Hans breaks out in a laugh that sounds fake and hurt and mean.

"And they told you that you had talent?" he asks, his one visible eyebrow lifted. "All the good journalists are probably dead or cripples like me." Small beads of sweat gather on his upper lip again. I collect the clippings and stuff them back into the box.

His laughter now fades into eerie wheezing before he stops. "I had talent once," he says. "I used to be a good watchmaker. I used to be good at repairing small, delicate things. Now I can't even hold still the one hand that I have left."

I look down at the table, trying to come up with something to say. Then I hear a key in the front door. Mama is coming home. What a relief! I don't have to be alone with my brother anymore.

thirty-four

Good morning." Hedwig greets me as she kneels in front of the oven to light the kindling. "Look at the gorgeous weather outside!"

Through the kitchen window I can see a rectangle of clear blue sky and the shingles of the houses on the other side of the yard glistening in the sunlight like mirrors.

"Have you seen Hans?" Hedwig asks.

"He has not come home," I say. "His bed is untouched. He left last night to visit his friends Otto and Robert."

"Maybe he slept over at Otto's," Hedwig says, rummaging through the coal box. Since I know that Otto is still in jail, I don't think Hans is at his house.

"What a glorious day!" Mama enters the kitchen with a basket in each hand.

"What's this?" I ask when she places them on the kitchen table.

"These are our leaflets with instructions for the workers of the AEG and Osram plants to go on strike," Mama says. "We have to go and distribute these now."

"Today is the day," Hedwig adds. "The revolutionary soldiers and sailors from the coastal areas are arriving in Berlin. In other cities the workers' and sailors' councils have already taken over. There will be a general strike." Hedwig waves at me with a red handkerchief. "When we go to bed tonight, things will have changed!"

"What about Oma?" I ask.

"I placed a tray with food next to her bed. She was still snoring when I went into her room," Mama says.

"I worry about Hans," I say.

"I worry that we'll have to face one of his anger outbreaks again later today," Hedwig says.

"He's still our brother," I say.

"When do you have to work today, Moritz?" Mama asks.

"I took the late shift, so I won't need to be at the printshop before five o'clock," I say.

"Could you please go and look for him at Otto's?" Mama asks. "He probably is fine and just got drunk with his friends, but we shouldn't let him out of sight for too long in his condition."

I nod. Mama now folds a red sheet before she places it on top of one of the baskets.

"This will be our red flag," Mama says. "Today, November 9, 1918, is an important day. The revolution is about to begin!" She beams at me.

"Let's go!" says Hedwig.

———✦———

At the streetcar station a woman informs me that the revolutionaries have cut the electricity cables of the overhead trains. The streetcar is out of service, but I don't mind the walk. This is one of those rare fall days when it is sunny and the air is cool and crisp. On my way I pass several trains stopped in their tracks. As I walk through the Tiergarten I startle a couple of boys who are sawing down a tree. They go right back to work when they realize that I am not a policeman. The police must have given up on charging wood thieves in search of heating fuel since not much is left from what used to be a lush forest in the city's largest park. The steel-blue metal statue of galloping horses on top of the Brandenburg Gate shines in the sunlight. The stolid horse of a lone taxi carriage parked next to the gate is trying to reach the leaves of a green wreath decorating the stone arch. Two policemen are posted next to the entrance of the Hotel Adlon, and I wonder why plush hotels are in need of protection. In front of the majestic building that used to house the Soviet Embassy a man sells postcards. I stop to look at his collection. He points to the many images of the Kaiser and says, "Take one of these. They will be more valuable once he is gone. And he soon will be! Right now I sell them for ten pfennig each." I buy three postcards with photos of the emperor and continue to walk up Unter den Linden Boulevard.

At the intersection with Friedrichstrasse the police have blocked automobile and carriage traffic, but pedestrians are allowed to walk through, and next to the opera house I pass a large group of workers marching toward the palace. They carry posters calling for the Kaiser to abdicate and for a socialist workers' government. "Bread and Peace!" I read on others. Some people wave red flags and all of them wear red handkerchiefs tied around their sleeves. I cross Alexander Square and pass City Hall, where I see more demonstrators approaching from the northern parts of town. I turn toward Nikolai Quarter and soon I have reached Otto's house. As I climb the stairs I remember my last visit, when they brought me here for the initiation. How much I wanted to be part of their group then.

Soon after my knock on the door I hear footsteps. The door opens and I look into the unshaven face of Otto's father. He is in his undershirt and his pants are hanging low on his waist, the top button open. "Who do we have here?" His voice sounds slurred.

"I'm looking for my brother, Hans," I say.

"Oh, you are the little rat that turned in my boy to the police," he says.

"Is my brother here?" I ask.

"He sure is," he says, and steps back, bending forward with a sweeping motion of his arm as if he were a butler opening a door for a dignitary. "Come on in, you little traitor."

I step inside, wondering if he will beat me for turning in his son, but I need to find Hans. "He's in the back," Otto's father calls, and disappears into the toilet out in the hall.

Hans lies on the sofa, his face scrunched on a pillow. "Hans," I call. "Wake up, Hans!" He opens his eye. "Oh," he groans. "What are you doing here?"

"I've come to take you home," I say. "Mama is worried about you."

"Isn't Mama busy overthrowing the government today?" he says, slowly getting up from the sofa. His patch has slipped off and I have to force myself not to stare at the raw hole where his eye used to be. But he catches my glance. "I'm no beau anymore," he says, arranging the eye patch over the empty socket. "The ladies won't like to look at this hole in my face either."

"Sorry, I don't have any breakfast." Otto's father is back with his hair slicked down with water, his cheeks freshly shaven. He tucks his shirt in and fastens a belt around his waist. "I have to go now and meet my regiment," he says.

"Are you still enlisted?" I ask.

"No," he says. "I came back from Russia last year. But I want to support the comrades that are coming from the outskirts. The Kaiser has to go and it is time for the war to end. Enough!"

"I can't believe you talk like that," Hans says.

"We discussed this last night," Otto's father says. "With lots of beer and schnapps."

"Yeah, plenty of that," Hans says, holding his head. "But I can't believe you want to support these Bolsheviks."

"I'm not supporting the Bolsheviks. This is Germany, not Russia. We want a democracy, elections, reforms." He makes a dismissive gesture. "But you are too stubborn to understand. Somebody has put the bug into your ear about Jews and Bolsheviks."

"You traitor," Hans says, but he smiles.

"The only traitor here is your brother," Otto's father says. "I know that my boy was up to no good, but *you* shouldn't have turned him in." He glares at me. "He told me about his plan with the ration cards when I saw him in prison. That was not a good idea, but you can't just rat on a friend like that."

I stare at the wooden floor.

"I'm going to have a word with him about that," Hans says.

"I'm leaving now," Otto's father says, putting his army tunic on. "You can still change your mind and join us."

"No thank you! Goodbye," Hans says. "And thanks for the schnapps and the bed!"

After we hear the door close we sit quietly for a while.

"Let's go home now," I finally say. "Mama worries about you."

"Why did you do this to my friends?" Hans asks.

"I couldn't falsify those cards. I didn't want to lose my job," I say.

"I can't believe you did this. Haven't I lost enough?"

"You haven't lost them," I say. "They will come out of prison and everything will be as it was before. You can continue stealing with them."

"You begged me to ask Otto to let you into the gang. Don't pretend you were surprised about what they did," Hans says. "I trusted you and you betrayed me."

"I had to do it. He blackmailed me, and I couldn't risk losing my work at the printshop."

"But Otto told his father that you wanted to protect your girlfriend, whose father owns a Jewish bookstore *and* was hiding weapons for the socialists!" Hans now sits at the edge of the sofa, shaking his head.

"She's not my girlfriend," I say. "She works for Hugo Haase, who helped to get Mama and Hedwig out of jail."

"My little brother gets a girlfriend, while I am being shot to pieces," he says with a mean laugh. "And you didn't even tell me about her."

"I was going to tell you, but then there never seemed to be a right time," I say.

"You put a Jewess over your friends," Hans says, and lets out a snort. With a dismissive gesture he pushes me aside and walks toward the door.

We leave the house without talking. By the time we reach the cathedral the square in front of the Imperial palace is filled with people. From Unter den Linden Boulevard more and more demonstrators are pouring in. The group of men and women closest to us carries a banner announcing a general strike at the Spandau ammunition factory. A little farther down the street a man holds a sign that reads "Don't Shoot, Brothers." Young boys have climbed up into the linden trees to get a better view, looking like bats holding on to the leafless branches. A car with a machine gun fastened on its roof gets stuck in the crowd.

"Hey, comrade," a soldier addresses Hans. "Take this off!" The man reaches for Hans's lapel and tries to rip off the black-and-white cockade of the Kaiser's army.

"Leave me alone," Hans calls, shoving the man with his left arm.

"Aren't you supporting the revolution, comrade?" the soldier asks.

"No," Hans says.

"These are the new times," the soldier continues, pointing to his red ribbon. "This is what you should wear on your lapel now. The red revolution has come."

But Hans pushes the man away. "I'm going home," he says to me, and disappears in the crowd.

thirty-five

Walking slowly through the stream of people, I make
my way along Unter den Linden toward Brandenburg
Gate. To protect their windows, most store owners have
closed the shutters, but the mood among the demonstrators is friendly. Soldiers call out the names of regiments
and garrisons that have joined the revolutionaries at the
outskirts of the city. Some of them carry their rifles, but
no shot is fired. Almost everyone has a red ribbon in his
or her lapel. I think of Hans's angry reaction when the
soldier tried to pin a ribbon on his and worry that if
someone did, there would be trouble. Near the Russian
Embassy a group of women march behind a banner that
says "Ludwig Loewe Munitions Works on Strike for Peace."
When they come closer I can hear them sing: ". . . comrades, come rally. And the last fight let us face. The

Internationale unites the human race." It's the same song that closes the gatherings Mama and Hedwig attend.

As I approach the Reichstag, a loud cheer erupts from a group close to the Bismarck monument when someone yells, "The Kaiser has abdicated!" A man next to me throws his hat in the air and a woman embraces her daughter. The people around me break into cheers, and soon I can see more hats being thrown in the air in front of the Reichstag, and, as the news travels farther through the crowd, more cheers echo from the Brandenburg Gate. "The Kaiser is no more!" an old man calls out, his face red from excitement. Here is the news all these people have been fighting and hoping for. The Kaiser has announced his resignation. I imagine Mama and Hedwig falling into each other's arms in celebration.

I scan the crowd and recognize the white mane of Wilhelm, Herr Haase's driver, in a group of men standing next to a line of official cars near the side entrance of the Reichstag. Wilhelm smiles when I approach him. "How are you, boy? Have you seen this?" He gives me one of the flyers announcing the Kaiser's abdication. "We got rid of the old bastard!"

"Yes, I know," I say, and when I put the paper into my pocket I feel the three postcards with the Kaiser's photo I bought earlier.

"Something is going on over there," he says, and points to a stream of people gathering at the stairs in front of the Reichstag. "I think it's the Social Democratic minister Scheidemann. Looks like he's about to give a speech."

An older man in a dark suit has thrown open a window in the Reichstag and waves his hand to quiet the crowd before he begins. "The old and decayed have fallen! The monarchy is shattered. Long live the new! Long live the German Republic!"

The audience cheers. I turn to Wilhelm, who is clapping his hands.

"Now we live in a German Republic," I say, wondering what exactly that will mean.

"This is a great day!" he says, and his smile makes the withered skin around his eyes crinkle. "I heard of some skirmishes near the palace and City Hall but the revolution was mostly peaceful."

"That's good," I say. "My mother and my sister are among the demonstrators somewhere in the city."

"I'm sure they are fine," Wilhelm says. "The comrades wouldn't let anything happen to them." He winks at me.

"What happens next? Will the social democrats form a government?"

"Good question," he says. "There will be a lot of fighting between the independents and the group around Ebert. Someone told me earlier that the Spartacist Liebknecht has already declared Germany a socialist republic from a balcony at the palace." He shakes his head. "The labor parties are divided. That's never good."

A tall man with a monocle and wearing the uniform

of a general leaves a side door of the Reichstag. Young soldiers intent on ripping the epaulets from his uniform immediately surround him. He tries to defend himself, but he can't push them away. They press him against the wall of the parliament building and only let him go after they rip his coat to shreds.

"You see," Wilhelm says, "it's not all peaceful, but it is men like him that we have to be most careful of. The generals hold the real power and won't let go of it easily."

Then he asks, "Did you come to see Rebecca?"

"Is she here?"

"She's inside the Reichstag with the boss," he says, pointing with his thumb to the wall of the parliament building behind us. "It must be busy as a beehive in there right now. Hugo Haase is negotiating with President Ebert about the formation of a new government. Exciting times!"

"Do you think I can go inside to see her?"

"They won't let you in without a pass," he continues. "The guards are very strict today because of all the commotion."

"I understand," I say, hoping that my face doesn't show my disappointment.

"But I'm sure you'll see more of her soon, you lucky man," Wilhelm says.

"What do you mean?" I ask.

"She likes you," Wilhelm says.

"Do you think so?"

"I know," he says.

"Did she tell you?" I hold my breath.

He chuckles. "She didn't need to. It's obvious."

I walk through the crowd past Brandenburg Gate and turn into Wilhelmstrasse where soldiers are posted in front of each of the ministry buildings. A group of women comes my way on the sidewalk, giggling and laughing. One of them stops, pulls a red ribbon from her pocket, and reaches for my collar. "This is such a remarkable day." She beams, and pins the ribbon onto my lapel. I see my reflection in a store window two blocks down and notice that I am still smiling.

thirty-six

When I arrive at the printshop, Old Moser is not there. It is unusual for him to be tardy, but since the subways aren't running and the streets are filled with demonstrators he might be held up and will come late. The editors have left material for a one-page special edition that I begin to read when I hear the sound of breaking glass from outside. But before I even reach the door a tall, skinny man in a sailor's uniform armed with a rifle enters the printshop.

"This printshop is seized by the revolutionary committee," he calls out, waving his rifle around the room. Two soldiers, also armed, follow him and position themselves next to the door, pointing their weapons at me.

"What do you want?" I ask.

"We want you to print the demands of the revolutionary committee," the sailor says.

"But the editors determine the content of the paper," I say.

"Those days are over!" the soldier guarding the door throws in. "There is a revolution in Germany, in case you missed it."

"We are reporting it," I say, and point to the editors' draft I have just started reading. "The Kaiser is gone and we live in a republic now."

"Are you making fun of the revolution?" the tall, skinny sailor says.

"I wouldn't dare," I say, and try to look as confident as this answer sounds.

"Then follow our instructions," the sailor says.

"I'm not going to just print what any of you tell me. This is a respectable newspaper," I say.

"How would you like us to set fire to all of this?" the soldier at the door says.

I look at the three men. Each one of them stares back at me with a hostile face. But I wouldn't dare to just print what they want without Old Moser here. Then I have an idea.

"I have to call my editor in chief," I say. Old Moser uses the new telephone in the printshop only rarely and I have never touched the machine. The soldiers' eyes follow me as I lift the receiver. I turn away from them so they don't see how worried I am. Will there even be an operator at work on a day like this? For what seems like a long time there is only silence on the line. Finally, I hear a woman's voice. "You're lucky. We just started to work again," she says, sounding as if she's speaking from very far away. I ask her to connect me with Herr Kirchner and after several click sounds he answers.

"We have a situation here in the print room. Members of a revolutionary committee want us to print an announcement and change the headline to 'Berlin Under the Red Flag.'"

"Are you alone?"

"Yes. Moser isn't here yet."

"What do you think?"

"I think we should do what they say. They're armed and are threatening to set the printshop on fire."

"Can you help them write the text?"

"You want me to help formulate the text?" I look at the tall sailor, who nods.

"Stay safe and I'll get there as soon as I can," Herr Kirchner says.

"All right," I say, and put down the receiver.

"Where is the draft of what you want us to print?" I ask the sailor.

"We don't have a draft, but we know what we want the article to say." He slings the rifle over his shoulder and steps closer to me. "You know how to operate the printing press?"

"Yes, I do," I say.

"You won't have to change the entire edition, just the first page," the sailor says. "My name is Erwin, by the way. Let's get started."

I walk over to the typesetting machine and start to

set the text according to his dictation. I make grammatical corrections where I see fit to ensure that the article will be published without any errors.

Herr Kirchner arrives just as I am printing the last ream. I am still standing behind the press and when Herr Kirchner lifts his hat in my direction I wave to him. I can see him talking to Erwin, both of them looking over the first page of the paper. I switch off the press, and with a last sigh the machine comes to a halt. I take the cotton out of my ears and walk over to Herr Kirchner.

"Moritz, my boy," Herr Kirchner says, and grabs my shoulders. "Thank you so much. I don't know what I would have done without you. You wrote a good first page, under pressure, all by yourself. We really needed someone with a cool head like yours!"

"I just did what I thought was right."

"Well, it was," he says, and holds up the evening edition.

Later, on my walk home, I am still brimming over from his compliments. When I recall the events of this extraordinary day my conversation with Hans throws a shadow over the memories. But then I think of Rebecca's beautiful face and Wilhelm's words replay in my head. *She likes you.* And I am floating again.

thirty-seven

Are you expecting someone for lunch?" I ask when Hedwig places a sixth plate next to the cutlery. The table is covered with a tablecloth and she has taken out the good china. It has been a while since we ate a meal from a festively set table.

"Aunt Martha will join us," Mama says. She places the white porcelain terrine next to the stove, where she has been stirring a soup since morning. Hans already sits at the table, his head down, studying today's paper.

"Is there a wedding?" Oma shuffles into the kitchen. "I hear church bells."

"Those bells mark the armistice. The war is over!" I say as I pull up a chair and help her to sit down.

"The war is over?" Oma asks. "Did the Kaiser announce a parade?"

"No," Hedwig says. "He abdicated and left Germany. He's not the Kaiser anymore. Remember? We told you yesterday."

"Ah," Oma says, and shakes her head. "That's all not true."

Aunt Martha's cheeks are red from the cold when she enters the kitchen. "Hello, everyone," she says. "Look what I brought!" She unwraps a loaf of bread.

"Is this real bread?" Hedwig asks.

"Yes, it is," Aunt Martha says. "My neighbor's son was part of the storming of the palace on Saturday. They found tons of flour in the Kaiser's pantry. It was distributed among the soldiers and workers. His mother baked bread and gave me a loaf!"

I take the loaf from her hands and put my nose close to the golden crust.

"Real bread, indeed," I say, inhaling the wonderful smell. I want to pass it to Hans, but he doesn't pay any attention.

"And I have more great news," Aunt Martha says. "The provisional government will give women the right to vote! They will announce it tomorrow. There will be elections for a National Assembly as soon as possible!"

"Wonderful," Mama says, and the women embrace each other. "You must be so happy after all these years of fighting for women's suffrage."

"You should be happy, too," Aunt Martha says. "Both of you. Even though Hedwig won't be allowed to vote. Voting age is twenty."

"You get to vote in a democratic election, Erma," Aunt Martha says to Oma.

"Why would I want to do such a thing?" Oma says.

"Because it's your right," Mama says.

Oma shakes her head and wraps her shawl tighter around her shoulders. She mumbles something that we don't understand.

"I think you should run for a seat in the National Assembly," Aunt Martha says to Mama.

"What? Me?" Mama asks, and puts her hand on her chest. "I don't know about that."

"I think that's an excellent idea," Hedwig says. "I am sure Hugo Haase will nominate you anyway. The party needs female candidates."

"For now let's just have some food," Mama says, and turns around to ladle the soup into the terrine.

Hans keeps his head down and continues to read the paper during lunch. I know that it annoys Mama, but she doesn't say anything.

"I wish we had something other than weak tea to drink so we could make a more festive toast," Aunt Martha says, holding up her cup. "But here is to the end of the slaughtering and the beginning of a new time for Germany." She looks at Hans, who doesn't move. Mama nudges him. "Drink with us."

"What should I drink to? The loss of my eye and arm? The death of many men, among them our father?" He looks angrily from Mama to Aunt Martha.

"Hans," Mama says. "I understand that you are angry and bitter. But it was not your fault that Germany lost the war. At the end, what counts is that you're alive and we are back together. And that there will be a new time. You have to look ahead."

"Have you read the conditions for the armistice?" he asks. "These conditions tell you what lies ahead. Humiliation! The allies didn't stop at demanding the Kaiser's abdication. They will keep up the blockade of our seaports and Germany has to hand over all its ships. The Rhineland will be occupied by foreign troops. All steel and coal industries in the Reichsland Alsace-Lorraine will become French. Germany has to surrender 5,000 guns, 25,000 machine guns, 150,000 railway coaches, 5,000 trucks, and more."

"But we lost the war," Mama says. "What do you expect?"

"You don't understand! It is a disgrace." Hans shakes his head and looks at me. "How come you don't say anything, Moritz?"

Suddenly, all eyes are on me. Even Oma looks in my direction.

"I think it's good that the war ended. The German army couldn't win it anymore. Too many soldiers died. Look what it did to you! It's better that it's over," I say, avoiding Hans's stare.

"Is that what your Jewess tells you?" he asks.

How dare he say this to me? I am so hurt I can't think

of a reply. Then Mama turns to him. "Hans," she says. "You are part of this family. And Papa and I taught you respect for others. Your brother didn't do anything to you. Stop hurting him!"

Hans puts his head down and nods slowly. The church bells are still ringing in the distance.

thirty-eight

We continue our meal in silence. I look at Hans but he keeps his head down, avoiding my glance. Just as I clean the soup bowl with the last bite of my bread the doorbell rings.

"Could you go and see who it is?" Mama asks.

I rush to the door, and to my surprise, Herr Goldmann stands on the doormat.

"You look like I just grew antennae," he says, and laughs. "Am I coming at a bad time?"

"No, no," I say. "We're just finishing our lunch. Come on in."

In the kitchen Herr Goldmann lifts his hat and introduces himself. "*Guten Tag!* I am Aaron Goldmann, an editor at the *Berliner Daily*." He looks from Aunt Martha to Mama. "And you are Moritz's mother."

"I am." Mama gets up and wipes her hands on her

apron. "This is my mother-in-law, my sister, Martha Ritter, my daughter Hedwig, and my son Hans."

"I'm sorry to interrupt your meal," he says, and bows to Aunt Martha and nods to Hedwig and Hans.

"We're finished," Mama says. "Moritz, please bring a chair."

"I'm here to thank your son," Herr Goldmann says.

"Please," Mama says, motioning him to take a seat.

"Thanks to Moritz's courageous act last Saturday the printshop of the *Berliner Daily* remained unharmed, and we managed to publish our evening edition without any problems. In the name of the editors, I would like to express my gratitude to Moritz."

All eyes turn to me but Herr Goldmann continues talking.

"And I also would like to offer Moritz a full-time position as a journalist at our paper," Herr Goldmann says.

I can't believe my ears. "Thank—you!" I stammer.

"That is great news, Moritz!" Mama says. "Congratulations!"

"Isn't this great!" Mama turns to Hans.

"Yes, it's wonderful," he says, but his voice doesn't sound enthusiastic. "A family of heroes!" he adds, and wipes his upper lip with the back of his hand.

Herr Goldmann gets up. "Well, that's all I wanted to say. Now I have to get back to work."

"Would you like to stay for coffee?" Mama asks. "It's

only chicory, no real beans, but made with hot water." She smiles.

"Thank you, some other time," he says. I walk Herr Goldmann to the door.

"Aren't you happy for your brother?" I hear Mama ask on my way back to the kitchen. "This is an accomplishment for someone who didn't study at university."

"I'm very proud," Hans says. "Moritz is a real hero. I just can't show it too much since I am still paying for my own heroic deeds to the Kaiser who you helped to chase away!"

I stop in the doorway. Why can't Hans be happy for me? I look at his stump and the patch over his eye and wait for the guilt to wash over me. But the familiar feeling doesn't come. Instead, I feel anger rising.

"I'm going out for a while," Hans says, and gets up. "Don't want to spoil your celebration."

"You already did!" I say. "You are spoiling pretty much everything around here."

He stops in his tracks and I can see the surprise in his eye.

"Really?" he asks.

"Yes," I say. "We're all tiptoeing around you. We'd like to help you. Mama gave you the name of a doctor. I offered to find you a job. But you refuse to accept our help. You need to see a doctor. You need to get better. But instead you are just making us feel guilty." The words stream out of me and I am afraid if I stop now I won't be able to say anything to him ever again. "I was looking forward to your return all this time. Now that you're back, I don't even know who you are anymore. I wonder if you do."

I take a deep breath, bracing myself for what he will say next. Hans turns around, and soon after the front door slams shut with a loud bang.

Mama buries her head in her hands.

thirty-nine

After a moment of silence Aunt Martha clears her throat and says, "He needs to see a doctor."

But Mama just shakes her head and says, "We've tried that."

"He is so mean now," Hedwig says. "I don't even want to be around him anymore. You never know when he will explode next. And all this talk about Jews. I don't know where he got that from."

"Yes, the Jews are now the scapegoats for everything," Aunt Martha says, shaking her head. "He's not the only one who says these things."

"The other night he started rambling about how I should stay away from Hugo Haase," Mama says. "I just don't know what to do!"

I listen quietly. Inside I bite back another surge of

anger toward Hans. When the women start to clean the table I grab my jacket and leave.

The city is cloaked in the freezing gray fog of late fall. It could snow today. When I hear the ringing of an approaching streetcar I hop on. It takes me eastward. I sit and stare out the window until I hear a voice asking me to leave the streetcar. I realize that the car has reached the end of the line. I cross the street and take the elevated train from Oberbaum Bridge back to the city center. There are still many soldiers in the streets, and in front of the Imperial Palace I see the remains of the barricades. Just before the streetcar rattles over the bridge I see a large bust of the Kaiser leaning upside down against a wall. A gash splits his forehead and a shard is missing from his cheek. I get off at Alexander Square and start wandering toward Nikolai Church.

I recognize him from a distance. The old Jew I sold the flour to sits on his stool, his wares spread out on that same black-and-white blanket. Two customers are leaning over the watches. They are wearing army jackets. Suddenly, one of them grabs the man and pulls him off his stool. The old man flails his arms in the air, but the tall soldier doesn't loosen his grip. Then the second man pulls the old Jew's corkscrew lock with one hand. I walk faster and when I come closer I can hear the old man screaming for help. The tall soldier lets the old man down and shoves him onto the blanket. Then I recognize the second soldier. The sleeve of his right arm is folded up and tucked into the shoulder. He wears a patch over one eye. He is laughing.

"Hans!" I call, and start running. "What are you doing?"

By the time I reach the old man the two soldiers have stomped off. I help him up and he slumps onto his stool. "Are you hurt?" I ask.

"Oh, boy! Thank God for your help!" He adjusts his yarmulke and pulls his coat straight. "My head hurts a bit. But thanks to you I'm fine. No blood, I think." He pats his forehead with a handkerchief.

"What did they want?" I ask.

"I don't know." He shrugs. "They just came, looked at the watches, and started swearing at me. They smelled like alcohol."

"I am sorry," I say.

"You called one of their names. Did you know him?" the old man asks.

"That was my brother," I say without looking at him.

"Your brother?" the old man says. "Which one was he?"

"The one with the patch over his eye."

"The pain," the old man says quietly. "It turned him into a wounded animal."

"We've tried to help him, but he doesn't want our help."

"No, no," the old man says. "You can't heal those wounds. You can only stay away."

The old man's words echo in my head as I walk home. *Stay away. Stay away.* How can I? By the time I reach our street the fog has turned the color of lead, announcing early dusk. I walk slower now, dreading that Hans might be home.

Just as I pass her floor, Frau Haller leaves her apartment dressed in black. She nods a greeting, and I remember what she told me when she received the notice about her son's death. *Be thankful your brother came home,* she said. I am not.

The apartment is cool and damp. Mama has been elected to one of the workers' councils and won't be back before late. We don't have enough wood or coal to keep the tile oven warm the whole day, and I can see Oma's breath when she greets me from her bed, where she is buried under a thick layer of blankets. I start the fire with the little wood left in the bottom of the coal box. I get my journal and, still in my jacket, begin to write. I describe how I felt when I saw Hans in the hospital, how sad I was on my way back, and how happy when we first hugged after he returned. It feels good to let the pen release the anger, to put the feelings into words. At the end of the page I quote Karl's drunken father, who from his bed behind the curtain in their small cottage said, "Depending how bad it hits you one is better off dead."

forty

Then I hear the door and Hans stumbles into the kitchen.

"Look who's here," he says. "My little brother, the poet."

"You've been drinking," I say. "You smell like alcohol." I get up and slip the notebook into my pocket.

"I had a few beers," he says. "I met my old companion Valentin von Ewald. He's back in the city."

"Is that the major you met in the hospital?"

"Yes, that very one. And look what he gave me." Hans pulls a revolver from his pocket. "That's the only thing I can hold steady, you see?"

He holds the revolver in my direction. His eyes look larger than usual and the sweaty patch on his upper lip glistens in the light of the gas lamp.

"Have you lost your mind? What do you need a revolver for?"

"Von Ewald wants to form a new group."

"What kind of group?"

"A group to restore dignity and order again in Germany," he says, and nods as if to underline the importance of what he just said.

"Dignity, by beating up old Jewish men, like I saw you do earlier?"

"You're just too dumb to understand." He makes a dismissive gesture.

"Too dumb to understand that you shouldn't have hurt the old man. Who's going to be in that group with you? Other mad veterans like you? Other morphine addicts?"

"Hey, hey, hey! Little brother! Be careful what you say! I'm the one with the gun here," he says, waving the revolver in the air.

"You wouldn't shoot your brother," I say.

"You can't know that. I've shot my share of men during the war." I catch the look in his eye and shudder when I can't find a speck of doubt.

"Speaking of m-m-morphine!" he continues, his words slurring. "I think you should come with me down to the pharmacy at the corner. I need more of my drug."

"Why would I do that? They are closed now, anyway."

"We will break in and take all of it from their cabinet in the back," Hans says.

"You're crazy!" I say. When I turn to leave I feel the mouth of the revolver in my back.

"You are coming with me!" Hans says, his voice now cold.

"No, I will not." I turn around and push the revolver down.

"Yes, you will! I thought you wanted to help me," he says, letting out a false laugh. His left arm is stretched out and he aims the revolver at my chest. "You owe me! You need to help me!" His one eye stares at me.

"I've tried that and you didn't want to be helped," I say, fighting the urge to look away. "I think you should leave us for good."

"What do you mean?"

"What will you do next? Shoot members of your own family because they work with Jews? Is that what's next?"

With a quick movement I grab the revolver from his hand.

"Why don't you go and stay with your friend von Ewald?" I ask.

"Give it back to me!" Hans yells, but my push makes him sway and he needs to steady himself against the table to find his balance. I leave. Before I reach the door I hear him yell after me, "Maybe that is what I'll do! Get away from *you!*"

Outside it has started to snow. For two blocks I walk briskly through the soft curtain of white, letting the cold air sting my lungs. At the next street corner I turn into a narrow side street and walk on until my breathing calms. There is a garbage bin in front of Palitzke's Paint Shop where I stop to look around in all directions. When I am sure that no one sees me I take the revolver out of my pocket, wrap it in an old newspaper someone has left in the garbage, and throw it into the bin.

As I return to our street I see Hans leaving the house. He carries his travel bag over his left shoulder and a suitcase in his hand. He doesn't notice me as he walks in the other direction. For a moment I want to call out after him. But then I stop, swallow the words, and remain standing on the sidewalk watching him grow smaller and smaller as he walks away.

"No, we didn't!" I say. But I can't look at her. Instead, I study the pattern of the tiles behind the stove. I won't tell Mama what Hans did to that old Jew. She doesn't need to know what a monster her son has become.

"Mama," Hedwig says, and places her hand on Mama's shoulder. "It was like living with a wild animal. We never knew what he would do next. And he was mean to us, even to you!"

"He was just so hurt," Mama sobs. "I should have taken better care of him."

"If this Valentin von Ewald is any friend at all, he might get him medical attention. Judging from the name and the address, he is a man of means," Hedwig says. "Maybe after some time we can contact him in Dahlem."

Mama blows her nose and dabs her face. She nods slowly and her eyes shift from Hedwig to me and back. "Now it's just us who have survived this horrible war," she says. She reaches out with one arm to take hold of my hand and pulls Hedwig closer with the other. "We have to stick together," Mama says quietly.

forty-two

I don't have to make up a pretense to see Rebecca, as I'm carrying a book from her father's library in my pocket. When I reach the bookstore the lights are still on, but the door is locked. I can see her inside and knock on the window.

"Hello," she says when she unlocks the door. She asks me inside. "We're just about to close. But come in."

"Thank you," I say. "I haven't seen you since the revolution, and I just wanted to see that you were all right."

"I am," she says. "No one in our group got injured."

The street lamp in front of the window throws a soft glow over Rebecca's beautiful face.

"What happened with your family?" she asks, and motions for me to sit next to her on a narrow bench in front of the shelves. "I saw your mother briefly in the Reichstag and she was happy."

"All is well with her," I say as I sit down. "But my brother..."

"What about him?" she asks, and I feel her hand next to mine on the bench.

"He got so angry at me, and then he had a revolver..." I say.

"He had a revolver?" she asks.

"Yes," I say. "He is sick. He's addicted to morphine and he thinks the revolution is a betrayal of the soldiers and the German people and..." I take a deep breath.

"Did he hurt you?" she asks.

"No," I say. I won't tell her what he did to the old Jew. "We had an argument and he left to stay with another war veteran in Dahlem. My mother is very sad about that."

Outside a bus honks, followed by the swishing sound of water splashed onto the sidewalk by thick tires.

"I'm glad nothing happened to you," she says, and I feel her hand slide on top of mine. I turn to her and she moves her face closer. Then the light comes on. "Rebecca?" her father's voice calls.

We both jump up from the bench. She straightens her dress and walks toward the back door. "Father," she says. "We have a visitor."

"Then what are you sitting in the dark for?" Herr Cohen asks, but when he sees me he smiles. "Oh, I see, it's Moritz."

He throws a quick glance to Rebecca, who averts her eyes.

"How wonderful you came to see us," Herr Cohen

says. "I would like to thank you for what you have done for our daughter. She told us that you have saved her from trouble twice now." He shakes my hand. "Why don't you come upstairs and meet my wife? Do you have a moment?" he asks. I nod, not sure if I have found my voice again.

He leads us upstairs into the family's living room. The walls of the hallway are lined with more bookshelves. When we enter the living room Herr Cohen calls for his wife. "Hannah, we have a visitor."

I can see the resemblance between Rebecca and her mother, the dark eyes, the thick hair, and straight posture. The hand Mrs. Cohen holds out for me to shake is as delicate as her daughter's.

"Have a seat." She motions to the sofa. "Let's have a toast, Nathan. Don't we have a bit of the port left?"

"Yes," he says, walking over to the hutch where he fills four glasses with a dark brown liquid. Mrs. Cohen offers me one and passes another to Rebecca, who has taken her seat next to me on the sofa.

"Thank you for helping our daughter," Herr Cohen says, holding up his glass. "Here is to a new time in Germany. May it be a peaceful time without the need to hide from the police."

". . . and a happy one," his wife adds, and we all touch glasses. I take a sip of the overly sweet wine and look at Rebecca. Our eyes meet and I wish we were alone again.

"But I need to go home now," I say, putting the glass on the end table next to me.

"We really hope to see you again soon, young man," Rebecca's mother says. "And I know my daughter wants to see more of you as well."

A smile darts over Rebecca's face.

"Yes," I say. "I will come back again soon."

forty-three

The next morning Old Moser is back for the early shift. When I enter the print room he greets me with a mock salute. "Good morning, hero of the revolution."

Mahlke shakes my hand. Turning toward Old Moser he says, "Leave the boy alone. He did the right thing. Thanks to him we still have a place to come to work."

"Yes," Old Moser says. "Because of your Spartacist comrades a workingman isn't even safe."

"The war is over. The Kaiser is gone. Germany is a republic!" Mahlke says. "These are great times for a workingman. Don't you agree, Moritz?"

"Yes," I say. "These are great times!" But Old Moser shakes his head before he clears his throat and spits into the wastebasket.

"What kind of republic are we?" he asks. "We still might end up in a Soviet-style state. A Council of People's

Representatives was elected at the meeting in the Circus Busch arena. They have soldiers' and workers' councils over there in Russia, too."

"But the majority of people want elections. They want the labor parties to unite and hold steady against the conservatives. I'm with Chancellor Ebert on this," Mahlke says. "He will bring us elections for a National Assembly and . . ."

The door opens and Herr Goldmann enters. "Good morning, gentlemen," he says. Old Moser and Mahlke walk over to the press and return his greeting with a nod.

"Has Moritz told you the news yet?" Herr Goldmann asks, and the two old men look at me.

"I haven't had time," I say. "We were just discussing the political situation."

"Well." Herr Goldmann motions them to come closer. "We have decided to offer Moritz a position as journalist at the *Berliner Daily*. He was a good printer, but he will make an even better journalist."

Mahlke breaks out into a broad smile. "I'll be darned," he says. "That little Moritz is going places. I knew there was something special up there." He taps his index finger against my forehead. Then he offers his hand. "Congratulations!"

Now we all look at Old Moser. "Say something, you old brick-head," Mahlke says, and nudges him in the side.

"I told your father that I would take good care of you," Old Moser finally begins. "If they think you can become a writer then it's probably true. I wish you good luck!" He shakes my hand. "And if the pale scribblers next door ever treat you badly, you know where you can find us!"

"We're only in the next building," Herr Goldmann says. "He's not going to leave the country. No reason to press the tear ducts." He puts his arm around my shoulders. "Let's go! There is work waiting for you!"

<hr />

"Welcome to your first day as a reporter for the *Berliner Daily.*" Herr Goldmann makes a sweeping motion with his right arm when we enter the office. Men tap at their typewriters and the drumbeat of their fingers fills the room.

"You don't look like someone who is just about to start a new career," Herr Goldmann says. "What's wrong? So sad to leave the print room?"

"I'm just thinking about my brother. He left us to move in with an old war buddy of his," I say. "We had another big argument, and he ended up waving a revolver at me."

"Sit down." Herr Goldmann motions to the swivel chair next to the empty desk that will be mine. "How did your mother take it?"

"He left her a note with an address in Dahlem," I say. "She was scared as well. But now at least we don't have to worry about what he will do next."

"War gives meaning to some men's lives. For other men, the experience of war extinguishes all meaning in life," Herr Goldmann says, and I feel tears welling in my eyes.

"I know," I say. "But I wish it wasn't like this."

"But you can't change things," Herr Goldmann says, passing me his handkerchief. "Try to remember him the way he used to be."

I dab my eyes and nod.

"You have your own life and have been thrown a big chance. Why not begin with your first writing assignment for our paper?" Herr Goldmann says, and cocks his head. "Are you ready to start work?"

"Yes." I nod and swallow. "Where do you want me to go?"

He smiles. "Your first assignment is to get your press credentials at the Reichstag, since we will ask you to observe the political events."

"All right," I say.

"Here." Herr Goldmann hands me a new notebook and three pencils. "These are your new tools. Carry them at all times!"

After I get a press pass from the Reichstag's Press Office that states my name and affiliation with the *Berliner Daily*, I don't want to leave the majestic building right away. Instead, I walk up to the visitors' gallery above the assembly hall and sit down on one of the wooden benches. Below me lies the elevated stage of the Reichstag's president with the speaker's podium in the middle. In the corner, next to the exit, I see Rebecca talking to a young sailor in uniform. He listens to her attentively and when he responds she laughs. They seem to know each other well. Now she touches his arm and leaves her hand on his sleeve while she looks at him, still talking. A bolt of jealousy jags through me. My arm seems to burn on the same spot where she has rested her hand on his. Who is he? I force myself to get up and quickly rush down the stairs. I don't want to watch this any longer.

Just as I turn into the large hall that leads to the exit doors, Rebecca walks from behind one of the pillars. The sailor is still next to her.

"What are you doing here?" Rebecca asks.

"I just got my press credentials. I'm now a journalist for the *Berliner Daily*," I say.

"Congratulations," she says. "That's wonderful news!"

"Thank you," I say, looking at the sailor.

"This is my cousin Daniel. He came here with the revolutionary sailors from Kiel, but now he wants to go back home. We were just saying goodbye," she says. "Daniel, this is Moritz."

"So you are the lucky one," he says, his eyes scanning me up and down. "Rebecca told me about you. You have captured my favorite cousin's heart. Take good care of it."

"Shhh." Rebecca frowns, and I can see her cheeks flushing red. "Don't say that!"

"I have to go," Daniel says, and gives her a hug. He shakes my hand and winks before he leaves.

"Are you still working with Hugo Haase?" I ask.

"Yes," she says. "But I'm now assisting him in his Reichstag office. I am here pretty much around the clock. We are so busy. Will you be reporting from the Reichstag?"

"That's what they want me to do," I say. "Should be exciting."

"I didn't know you were also a writer," Rebecca says. "Maybe you could help me look over a press release. It's due at noon so I don't have a lot of time."

"What is it about?"

"Hugo Haase is arguing with Ebert about who should have control over the police and military. He wants to make sure everyone knows the position of the Independent Social Democrats. It needs to be short and precise. Do you think you can help?" she asks.

"I can try," I say.

"But I am warning you. It's a madhouse up there. People barge into the office all the time with questions nobody knows the answer to," she says.

"No problem," I say, and as we walk toward the stairs I wonder when I will ever see her alone.

forty-four

Mama has decided to become a party candidate for the first National Assembly. The election is scheduled for January of next year. On a Saturday afternoon at the beginning of December the party delegates for Mama's district meet to select their candidate. To be there when Mama gets elected, I have to hurry after work. By the time I reach Fox's Pub, Hugo Haase has just finished his speech. ". . . and that's why I think that Anna Schmidt will make a marvelous member of the first democratically elected National Assembly in Germany." The hall is unheated and only the first two rows of seats are occupied by delegates. Mama sits next to the podium together with the other candidate for the position. She looks radiant, even wrapped in her coat and shawl, and I am proud of her. The delegates put their ballots into a basket and a woman takes the basket to a group of party members at the back of the stage who will count the votes. Rebecca is one of them and I wave to her when our eyes meet. There are not too many votes to count and soon a woman comes back to the front and hands Hugo Haase a note. He walks up to the podium and declares: "Anna Schmidt has received thirty-five of forty-four votes. She will represent this district for the Independent Social Democrats in the upcoming election to the German National Assembly." He turns to Mama. "Congratulations!" he says, and shakes her hand. "I'm glad that you decided to do this! The party needs women like you."

The people in the audience applaud; many of them stand up. I join them in their standing ovation, clapping my hands until they throb.

Mama is surrounded by well-wishers and I wait my turn to give her a hug.

"Congratulations!" I say when we embrace. "I'm very proud of you."

Hedwig gives Mama a red carnation. "That's the only one we could find," Hedwig says. Mama gives her a hug and fastens the blossom onto her lapel. Aunt Martha opens her arms to embrace Mama and when she lets her go she says, "We should go to Josty's and celebrate. The evening is on me, ladies!"

Most members of the audience are hurrying toward the door, but I stay back while the women around Mama and Aunt Martha get ready to leave. I am afraid that

Rebecca will join them, but she is still cleaning around the table on the stage. As I linger in the corner, I watch her take the red cloth off the table and slowly fold it.

"Are you coming with us, Rebecca?" Mama asks.

"No," she calls. "I'll finish up here. You go ahead."

Hedwig pulls her shawl around her neck, but before she walks out the door she turns around and says, "Moritz will be soooo happy to help you!"

I want to make a face at her, but she has already closed the door behind herself.

Rebecca steps down from the stage. "Do you need any help?" I ask.

"No, I think it's all done," she says, and I can see her breath in the chilly room.

"Aren't you proud of your mother?" Rebecca asks. "This is such a wonderful result for her."

"It sure is," I say, trying not to stare too much at the cute dimple in her cheek.

"You know that Hugo Haase has asked me to assist your mother in her election campaign?" Rebecca asks.

"That's very good news for my mother," I say.

"You could join us. You could help write her speeches. We could work on them together sometimes," she says.

"Yes, we can," I say, and for a moment our eyes are locked and I am not cold anymore.

Suddenly the lights go out and we are standing alone in the dark hall. A small panic jolts up from my stomach as I wonder whether I should take her hand now, if this is the time to kiss. But then a voice calls out from the other end of the room, "Are you two still in here? I'm about to lock the door."

"Wait!" I answer. "We were just leaving."

We hurry outside, where icy wind greets us, and we huddle close to the building. Rebecca pulls her scarf tighter before she buries her hands in the pockets of her coat. I take a deep breath and suggest, "Let's walk down to Friedrichstrasse and find a coffee shop." She nods and we pass half a block without talking, our shoulders hunched against the cold.

"Daum's Café is closest from here," she says when it starts to snow.

"That's a good idea," I say.

"We'll get the coffee faster if we take the streetcar," Rebecca says, and points to one waiting at the corner. We step quickly inside and sit down on a bench in the back. The snow is falling heavier now, and thick flakes melt, sliding down the windowpanes. There are no other passengers. Rebecca leans her head against my shoulder. I put my arm around her and bury my face in her hair. We are finally alone.

forty-five

On the last Saturday before Christmas, I meet Rebecca at the Börse subway station.

"Bad day to begin an election campaign," I say. "I wish they had waited with the voting until spring. It is too cold to hand out pamphlets."

"They couldn't have waited. We need a democratically elected parliament as soon as possible," Rebecca says, and pulls a piece of paper out of her pocket. "Look what I found today." She unfolds a flyer that reads:

Our Fatherland is in Danger. It is threatened not from the outside, but from the inside, by the Spartacus Group. Kill their leaders Karl Liebknecht and Rosa Luxemburg and you will have Peace, Work, and Bread.

"This is terrible," I say, and stare at the name of the group that posted it, the Organization of Front Soldiers.

"They are correct that our fatherland is in danger," Rebecca continues. "But it's people like this who threaten it with their hatred of socialists and Jews."

As we walk toward the exit, over the rattle of the trains, I add in a low voice, "And I think my brother is one of them."

Wet snow covers the square in front of the cathedral and our steps leave brown imprints in the slush. Rebecca takes out a woolen scarf, covers her hat with it, and ties the ends around her chin.

"You look like you have a toothache," I say.

"If I don't do this I'll have an earache," she says.

"Let's go through the Christmas Market," she suggests, and points toward the boardwalk near the canal where only a few booths are lined up. Vendors sit wrapped in blankets in front of their wares. Since the blockade of German harbors still continues, most of the stalls' offerings resemble only the usual black market merchandise—clocks, silverware, wool, and felt material to make coats. A girl sells gingerbread horses. I look at Rebecca, but before I can even ask if she would like one she shakes her head. We pass a woman who tries to keep warm by blowing into her gloves in front of a tray of homemade Christmas ornaments. An old organ grinder with a felt cap plays "O Tannenbaum" on his organ, but the atmosphere is more gloomy than festive.

"Not much to buy here," Rebecca says.

"And there aren't too many people out here we could convince to vote," I say. "We're almost alone on the street."

"What did you say?" she asks. I pull the scarf off her ear and put my lips right next to it before I say, "Nobody here to present our convincing arguments to." Then I cover her ear again, leaving a light kiss on the cold skin.

"That tickles," she says, and giggles before adjusting her scarf.

"Let's go to Leipzigerstrasse. There will be more people we might persuade to vote for Anna Schmidt," I say.

"We could also paste some of the flyers onto advertisement pillars," she says as we cross Gendarmenmarkt. "I brought the glue."

"Looks like somebody else has been doing that already," I say, and point to a wall that is plastered with flyers. We step closer to read them. In large bold-print letters they call out: GERMANS! DON'T VOTE FOR JEWS!

"Oh my God." Rebecca turns to me, suddenly pale.

"Those bastards," I say.

"I think it's those two over there," she says, and points to the other end of the street, where two men have just finished wiping a brush over a poster before they step back from the wall.

"Let's just go back and hand out our pamphlets near the gate," she says. "I don't want to get any closer to them."

Before heading off I turn to take another look at the two men plastering the posters. Rebecca waits for me,

Author's Note

The fall of 1918 was an important turning point in German history. The German Reich's military defeat sparked a revolution that swept away the monarchy and gave Germany a new, democratic government. I tried to imagine what it might have been like for a teenage boy who had grown up in the Wilhelmine Empire and whose father had died in the war to witness the collapse of the old, familiar regime, the departure of a monarch he had once admired, and the military defeat of his proud country.

In August 1914, when the troops left Berlin for the border with Belgium and France, they were enthusiastically sent off by cheering crowds. Kaiser Wilhelm II gave a confident speech, assuring his soldiers that they would come back "before the leaves have fallen from the trees." But the trees lost their leaves four times before the war ended.

Four years of war took a heavy toll on the civilian

population, particularly in German cities. While most able men were fighting at the front, the war economy demanded the production of weapons and ammunition, forcing women to work in factories. The British naval blockade of German seaports restricted the supply of raw materials and food. The German government responded with a rationing system, resulting in a thriving black market and the city population's so-called hamster-tours to the countryside in search of food. The naval blockade also impeded the import of fertilizer and, as a result, from 1916 onward basic agricultural staples like potatoes, grain, and meat became scarce. Germans used ersatz products such as "war bread," milk powder, and coffee made from chicory. The particularly harsh winter of 1916/1917 became known as "turnip winter," when a premature frost destroyed the potato harvest and the turnip, which didn't suffer frost damage, became the main food source.

The Social Democratic Party of Germany (SPD) was considered the leader of the European socialist movement and after the elections of 1912 made up the strongest faction in the German parliament. But tensions about Germany's participation in the war grew among the party delegates, and when the left-wing pacifist group, led by Hugo Haase, denied authorization of additional war bonds to finance the war, they were expelled from the SPD. In April 1917, the Independent Social Democratic Party (USPD) was founded, with Hugo Haase as its chairman. The Majority Social Democrats (MSPD) remained the dominant political force under their leader, Friedrich Ebert, who feared a revolution and hoped for reforms of the political system through negotiations with the monarch and the Imperial Chancellor, Max von Baden.

An even more radical leftist group of former SPD members, under Karl Liebknecht and Rosa Luxemburg, founded the Spartacus League. These Marxists hoped Germany would follow Russia's example, and they agitated for a revolution under the leadership of workers' councils. In December 1918, the Spartacus League was officially named the Communist Party of Germany (KPD).

At the end of October 1918, the sailors' refusal in the coastal city of Wilhelmshaven to follow an order to launch a last, hopeless attack on British ships sparked a mutiny that quickly spread across the country and grew into what became known as Germany's November Revolution. Workers' and soldiers' councils formed spontaneously and took over power in most German cities.

On November 9, 1918, the Kaiser abdicated and fled to Holland. After the Imperial Chancellor announced the Kaiser's abdication, Philipp Scheidemann, a majority social democrat, proclaimed the republic from a window of the Reichstag. Shortly after, Spartacist Karl Liebknecht announced the "Free Socialist Republic." This double proclamation of a German republic illustrates the underlying conflict between the social democrats and socialists.

For a short time Friedrich Ebert and Hugo Haase both became members of a provisional government, but the cooperation between independent and majority social democrats ended in December 1918 over disagreements regarding the future course of the revolution.

The election of January 1919 brought a clear victory for the Majority Social Democrats, and Friedrich Ebert became the first democratically elected Chancellor of the German Reich. The Independent Social Democrats won only about 7 percent of the votes. Both social democratic parties had nominated women, some of whom became members of the Reichstag. The parliament moved its sessions from Berlin to Weimar to mark a visible break with old autocratic tradition.

At the end of World War I anti-Semitic activities became more frequent in Germany. Even though Jews made up less than 1 percent of Germany's population, they became handy scapegoats. Rumors claimed that Jewish businessmen had enriched themselves during the war and Bolshevism was made out to be a Jewish movement. From November 1918 onward, anti-Semitic flyers could be found around the city, some of them explicitly calling for the murder of the communist leaders Rosa Luxemburg and Karl Liebknecht.

Conservatives and ex-military leaders criticized the armistice agreement and later the Treaty of Versailles, blaming socialists, communists, and Jews for Germany's defeat. They claimed that a lack of public support had caused Germany to lose the war. This opinion, known as the "stab-in-the-back legend," continued to flourish among anti-democrats, conservatives, and embittered war veterans. Their frustration cast a dark shadow over the Weimar Republic and helped to pave the way for the rise of Adolf Hitler.